*Come Helen High Water*

**Also by Susan McBride**

**River Road Mysteries**
*Not a Chance in Helen*
*Mad as Helen*
*To Helen Back*

**Debutante Dropout Mysteries**
*Say Yes to the Death*
*Too Pretty to Die*
*Night of the Living Deb*
*The Lone Star Lonely Hearts Club*
*The Good Girl's Guide to Murder*
*Blue Blood*

**Women's Fiction**
*The Truth About Love & Lightning*
*Little Black Dress*
*The Cougar Club*

# Come Helen High Water

## A River Road Mystery

### SUSAN McBRIDE

WITNESS
IMPULSE

*An Imprint of HarperCollinsPublishers*

This is a work of fiction. Names, characters, places, and incidents are products of the author's imagination or are used fictitiously and are not to be construed as real. Any resemblance to actual events, locales, organizations, or persons, living or dead, is entirely coincidental.

COME HELEN HIGH WATER. Copyright © 2017 by Susan McBride. All rights reserved. Printed in the United States of America. No part of this book may be used or reproduced in any manner whatsoever without written permission except in the case of brief quotations embodied in critical articles and reviews. For information, address HarperCollins Publishers, 195 Broadway, New York, NY 10007.

Digital Edition JUNE 2017 ISBN: 978-0-06-242795-3
Print Edition ISBN: 978-0-06-242797-7

WITNESS logo and WITNESS IMPULSE are trademarks of HarperCollins Publishers in the United States of America.

HarperCollins is a registered trademark of HarperCollins Publishers in the United States of America and other countries.

FIRST EDITION

17 18 19 20 21   HDC   10 9 8 7 6 5 4 3 2 1

*For my father, who is living with Alzheimer's
and can no longer read the books I write.*

*Before the Flood*

## Chapter 1

---

*Sunday*

THE "WALK OF shame," wasn't that what they called it?

Despite the hangover that played timpani drums in her head, Luann Dupree cracked a smile as she locked her car and scurried toward her front door in the gray light of early morning. She'd always been such a straight arrow that it tickled her to envision herself being labeled a hussy. Unfortunately, it appeared that no one was around to witness her predawn homecoming.

She glanced right and left, checking an all-but-deserted Main Street beneath the still-glowing streetlamps. It felt very much like a ghost town, though there were a few signs of life: the lights flickering on at the diner down the block; a whip-poor-will calling out from a nearby tree; and a cat with a bell on its collar darting beneath a parked car. Otherwise, the town slept, not to awaken until the morning newspaper landed hard upon front porches.

"No one here but us chickens," she murmured, shaking her head.

She let herself into the building that had, half a century ago, been the Spring Creek Hotel. Through the years the hotel had fallen into disrepair. When its owners died and their heirs placed it on the market for a pittance, the town council had scooped up the property for the River Bend Historical Society. Walls had been torn down to create vast space on the first floor for a museum. The second floor held countless documents and photographs that needed scanning into the system. Its unoccupied rooms also provided storage for the dozens of boxes found in the attic during the renovation and an extensive inventory of items left to the Historical Society by deceased town residents.

The renovation had been fully completed a year ago, and Luann was still sorting through the jumble.

She'd assumed the helm of the Society a decade before and had spent so much time in the building that it felt like home. Heck, it *was* her home. Before the town council had pushed forward plans to turn the attic into a tiny one-bedroom apartment, she'd often slept on the couch in her office. Though her brand-new living space was hardly bigger than a breadbox, it was all that she needed, seeing as how she was single without even a pet to her name.

One of these days, Lu imagined moving into a cottage perched atop the bluffs above the Mississippi River. How glorious it would be to wake up every morning and see the sunrise dapple the water! It would be even better if she had someone to share it with, she mused wistfully.

Not that there was anything wrong with living alone. Luann had been alone most of her fifty-two years. If she'd liked pets, it might have been a different story. But she was bored to death of herself and itched to share her passion with someone else, hopefully before another decade passed her by while her nose was buried in census tomes or dusty old photographs.

*"It's never too late in life to have a genuine adventure."*

Lu thought of the quote from an author whose book about pirates she'd devoured. When had she experienced a genuine adventure? When had she just thrown caution to the wind and let go?

She felt like all she did was dig into the past and discover *other* people's adventures. But what she did mattered, she reminded herself. Uncovering the past and telling its stories was important for future generations. What she left behind as director of the Historical Society—the artifacts, the books, letters, diaries, and photographs—they lived on. They were her progeny.

Maybe it wasn't the same as having a family and raising children to unleash on the world, but it had to be enough.

With a sigh, she hesitated in front of the antique hall tree that sat inside a small foyer just off the main entrance. She stared at her weary face in the mirror and attempted a smile.

Her chin-length bob looked disheveled. Her eyes

were puffy and underscored by melted mascara. Her lipstick hadn't lasted through her third martini, much less one passionate kiss.

She had turned into a lightweight in her middle age, she decided. She used to be able to handle her liquor without having to be put to bed like a child. Try as she might, she could hardly remember a thing from the night before beyond sitting at the bar and flirting with her newfound beau. It was a very good thing that he had been such a gentleman, or she could have ended up in dire straits.

"You're not very adept at playing the party girl," she told herself and winced.

She was already dreading having to entertain the volunteers who would show up at the Historical Society later that morning. Perhaps she'd stay in bed and put a *Do Not Disturb* sign on the locked front door. Still, she had her doubts that they'd go away. Most of the townsfolk she dealt with were hardly the mousy live-and-let-live types. They were kind, yes, but bossy and prone to interfering in everyone else's business.

How they would love to hear what she'd been up to last night! If she dared to spill the beans, they'd have enough fodder for the grapevine to carry them through the next week, even longer if they were to learn that she'd met her paramour online and their romance had blossomed via texts, e-mails, and secret Facebook messages. To modern-day daters those things were the norm. To the widows of River Bend, of which there were plenty, such newfangled ways of courtship were distasteful at best and suspect at the very least.

But Luann wasn't about to share all her secrets. She had grown up in this tiny Illinois river town. She knew how things went. So ten years ago when she'd moved back to River Bend from St. Louis to take over the Historical Society, she'd done her best to keep her private life private.

Mostly.

She wasn't big on trust, particularly where women were concerned. It seemed like the single ones were usually jealous and the married ones judgmental. If she had to call anyone her best friend, it would be Sarah Biddle. Luann had known her since grade school. Besides, who better to keep tabs on her than the sheriff's wife, just in case her Internet beau turned out to be Jack the Ripper? Though she hadn't confided much about her online relationship to Sarah, she had told her about The Date.

"Let me go with you to meet this guy. I'll keep my distance so I don't scare him away," Sarah had offered. "What if you get catfished?"

Lu had laughed. "The only catfish in my plans are the fritters at the Loading Dock."

Sarah had frowned. "You're not taking me seriously."

"Give me some credit," Lu had told her, squeezing her hand. "I'll be fine."

"Says every woman in every horror movie who goes into the dark basement when they hear a bump in the night, and what happens to them?" Sarah had prodded with an anxious look on her long face. "That's right," she had finished, not waiting for Lu to answer. "They end up shish-kabobbed and eviscerated."

"Then it's a good thing I'm not meeting him in a dark basement," Luann had replied, adding a silent *Thanks for the reassurance, pal.*

As if she hadn't been nervous enough.

She'd quieted the somersaulting butterflies in her belly with beer, sipping a bottle as she prepared for her date. She'd even considered backing out at the last minute, only to remind herself, *What the heck have you got to lose?*

Besides, she and Mr. Maybe had agreed to meet in a public place, which made Luann feel safe enough. If she didn't like him in person, she could always leave.

As it turned out, Lu and Mr. Maybe had hit it off so well face-to-face that she'd overindulged in the dirty martinis he kept insisting on buying her. She couldn't remember much besides waking up in a room at the Ruebel Hotel—alone—and hoping she hadn't screwed up her chance at love by passing out. She'd still had her clothes on, which was mostly a relief, and she hadn't been robbed. She'd stopped at the front desk to ask if Mr. Maybe had gotten a room for himself, but he'd only paid for hers and left her a note: *Take two aspirin and text me in the morning.*

Ha!

She considered texting him now, but got caught up in a yawn.

*Don't text him yet,* she told herself.

She didn't want to seem too desperate.

First she planned to follow his advice and take two aspirin. She'd chase them with a full glass of water and a few hours' sleep. *Screw the volunteers,* she decided and turned toward the stairs that led up to her apartment. She reached for the banister but paused, detecting a whiff of something funky in the air.

Had an animal died in her office?

She headed toward the rear of the building, searching for a source of the malodor that made the timpani drums in her head turn even louder.

The renovation notwithstanding, the Victorian structure could be a headache with its terribly creaky floors—which she'd insisted on saving—and basement so dark and moldy that the town council had moved the furnace and water heater into a room at the back of the building. After clearing out anything of value from the maze of rooms below, Luann had padlocked the basement door, refusing to descend the stairs again, even under threats of a tornado. But it wasn't mildew that caused her to pinch her nose now.

"Good Lord, what is that?" she asked herself.

Usually the air bore the delicate scent of the lavender bubbles she bathed in—to disguise the mustiness of the historical texts she was always reading for research—but instead it reeked of muck and fish and nasty Mississippi River mud.

Lu strode through the rooms that ran shotgun

through the building. She bypassed framed nineteenth-century plats of River Bend, shelves holding precious donations of Native American pottery, and catalogued boxes filled with arrowheads from the tribes that had been the region's first inhabitants.

When she reached the rear of the building and entered the office, she instantly realized the source of the stink, and it wasn't pretty. Brown water had seeped beneath the back door, creating a puddle on the pickled pine floor. Fleetingly, she thought, *Oh, God, the creek is rising awfully fast. Better ask the mayor for sandbags.*

But what disturbed her more was the unlocked door and a vague trail of damp. Were those footprints?

This was not good, she told herself. Not good at all.

Had someone broken in while she was gone?

For a split second Luann freaked out, until she reminded herself that she'd left what mattered most in good hands.

Feeling calmer, she checked the lock, but there were no signs of tampering: no gouges from a screwdriver or broken pane of glass. Had she been so discombobulated when she'd left for her date that she'd forgotten to lock up? Hastily, she turned the dead bolt, her heart pounding in sync with the throb at her temples.

She glanced around her office but could find nothing amiss. No drawers opened or files rifled through. She backtracked through the building, flipping on the lights in the rooms housing artifacts and texts. Though she squinted at every case full of arrowheads and stone tools, ran a finger along the weathered spines of shelved books, and inspected the pottery, everything looked as she'd left it.

"Whew." She let out a sigh of relief, feeling weak at the knees.

If anyone *had* come inside—perhaps a nosy councilman with the spare keys checking up on her work—they certainly hadn't stayed long. River Bend was not the kind of place where crime ran rampant, at least not beyond cars running stop signs and petty disagreements flaring up among neighbors.

She took great care to turn the dead bolts before she clutched the banister, made her way upstairs to her apartment, and fumbled her way inside. The pale pink of the dawn sky filtered in through the blinds as she went to the galley kitchen and popped two aspirin, then chased the pills with a full glass of water.

En route to her bedroom, she heard the crunch of tires on gravel and a familiar thud against the front door.

*Paperboy,* she thought, though he wasn't a boy, was he? He was a grown man with a full-size beard that brought to mind soldiers in Civil War–era photographs. Strange how that trend had come back after all these years, or maybe it was fitting considering the political climate.

Luann still wasn't sure if she was pro or con, considering how kissing a bewhiskered man meant inevitable beard burn.

Absently, she touched her lips and smiled to herself.

She passed beneath the arch leading into the bedroom, kicking off her shoes. As she began shrugging out of her sweater, the table light switched on, blinding her for an instant.

"Hey, sweetheart," a soft voice said from the far corner.

Luann blinked away the floaters, eyes widening as a man rose from her bedside armchair.

"Wh-What are you doing here?" she sputtered, noticing the opened drawers in her bureau and the suitcase on her bed. "Were you looking for something?"

"No." He smiled. "I was packing your things."

Packing her things?

"How did you get in?" she asked, pressing a hand to her chest and hoping she didn't have a heart attack.

He didn't answer her question. Instead he reached a hand out to her. "You told me you were ripe for a real adventure. So let's do it, Luann. Let me take you away."

"Away?" she asked, her pulse scudding in her ears. "To where?"

"Leave it to me," he said. "I'll take care of everything."

Luann froze for an instant, about to tell him he was a fool, that she wasn't about to go anywhere with him. But she caught herself before she did.

*It's never too late in life to have a genuine adventure.*

What if this was her last chance?

What if he wasn't just Mr. Maybe, but Mr. Right?

How would she know if she didn't take that leap of faith?

Luann suddenly forgot how tired she was and how her head ached. She ignored all common sense, brushing aside any questions or doubts.

"Let's do it," she said, her voice quiet but firm.

Then she threw herself into his arms, and he held on to her so tightly she couldn't breathe.

## Chapter 2

ELLEN ASHBY STOOD in her kitchen, slicing red onions for a tossed salad. She was fifty-four but looked ten years younger in flip-flops and cropped jeans, rolled up at the cuffs. She was babbling nonstop about enrolling her twelve-year-old daughter in hip-hop dance class and how she wasn't sure if the girl would survive because of her two left feet.

"You know what a klutz Sawyer is," she said with a laugh and used the back of her hand to brush aside a wisp of gray-streaked brown hair that had escaped her ponytail. "It was such a relief when she quit gymnastics. I thought for sure she'd break her neck on the balance beam."

Bernie Winston shifted in his seat.

"Remember how I was at that age, Dad?" she went on, making circles in the air with a paring knife. "I fancied myself a prima ballerina. I would twirl and twirl until I fell down, dizzy. You used to say I was a whirling dervish."

*A whirling dervish?*

What the devil was that?

Bernie wrinkled his forehead, befuddled. He tried hard to focus on what she was saying but his mind kept losing track midsentence. He looked around him, and his hands clenched to fists in his lap.

"You want something to drink, Dad? It's pretty warm out there for April," the woman said. "I've got ice water, tea, and beer." She laughed nervously. "Wait, nix the beer. Mom would have a fit if she saw you drinking liquor." At his quizzical stare, she added, "You can't have alcohol with your meds."

His meds?

Bernie wanted to ask what she was talking about and rubbed his whiskered jaw, which got him to wondering how he'd forgotten to shave. He used to do it every morning without fail. Though he had gotten up extra early today so he could get on the road, hadn't he? That was probably it.

"Dad?"

She stared at him, worry plain on her face. Her concern tugged at something inside him. Bernie wasn't sure why he felt the need to apologize, but he gave it a shot anyway.

"I'm sorry. I'm just so tired. I spent the day driving across the state," he said, giving his neck a roll. He could feel the tension in his shoulders. "I was inspecting the Northern Illinois mines for Peabody. I hardly had time to stop for lunch."

"Inspecting the mines for Peabody?" Ellen repeated, scrunching up her face. She turned off the tap and wiped her hands on a dish towel. "But you haven't worked for them for at least twenty . . ." She stopped herself, biting on her bottom lip. "Are you okay, Dad? You do look tired," she said, coming near. "Sure I can't get you some water?"

"No, no water." He waved her off, feeling a sudden sense of panic. "This isn't my house, is it? I want to go home."

"It's okay, Dad. You're in my house," the woman said calmly. "You and Mom came for dinner."

Bernie squished his eyes closed. A picture filled his head, of the only kitchen he remembered. It had floral-patterned linoleum, a red Formica table and chairs, a gingham skirt on the porcelain sink, and his mother with her cropped blond hair and pale eyes, offering him a warm chocolate chip cookie.

He opened his eyes and looked around him. He realized this wasn't that place. This wasn't any place he knew, was it? It was all stainless steel, white cabinets, and granite, as sterile as a hospital. Was that where he was? Was he in a hospital?

"Where's Mother?" he asked.

"Do you mean *my* mother or your mother?"

He squirmed, gaze darting about.

"My wife, she drove me here," he muttered to himself. "She was with me today, visiting the mines. I need to be resting. I'm worn out . . . I need to go home."

"That does sound tiring," the woman said, and Bernie refocused on her. The anxiety in her face seemed to disappear, and she smiled sympathetically. "So Mom went with you to the mines today, did she?" she asked and crouched low so they were eye to eye.

Bernie blinked. "My wife was with me. She drove me all over the state."

"But now Mom's outside talking to Sawyer while Matt grills our burgers. You did say you wanted a cheeseburger, right?"

"Mom?" he repeated, and he put his hands on either side of his face. "Who is Mom?"

"My mother, the person who gave me life," the woman told him, speaking slowly and very loudly, as though he were hearing impaired. "She's your wife, Betty Winston."

Bernie dropped his hands to his lap. "Yes, of course, Betty's my wife." He sighed, suddenly hearing a murmur of voices beyond the French doors, but he didn't move from the chair. He didn't always know which end was up—or who was who—but he knew hot from cold. Outside felt like an oven. Inside, cool air surrounded him. He didn't feel like moving.

He squinted at the woman, trying to place her. She reminded him of someone, but he wasn't sure who.

"I drove all over the state today, inspecting mines." He rubbed a hand over his brow. "Whew, and it was hot."

"Yes, you told me about that already," the woman said softly. "Sure I can't interest you in some iced tea, Dad?" She crouched before him, and there were tears in her eyes. "Tell me what you need, and I'll get it."

"No, thank you, I'm fine." He waved her off as she peered at him, waiting. He could tell she was a sweet lady, genuinely caring. He was certain he knew her, but her name escaped him. They were related somehow, weren't they? Was she his sister, or his niece, perhaps? That idea that she wasn't a stranger made him relax. He nodded at some photographs on the wall of a girl with a gap-toothed grin and braids.

"She's a lovely child," he said, trying to make conversation. He was pretty good at that for an engineer.

"She's smart, too, like her grandpa." The woman put a hand on his knee.

"So she's yours?" he asked.

"Yes, she's mine," the woman replied. "Her name is Sawyer. She's your granddaughter."

"Hmm," Bernie said because nothing else came to him. He felt no connection to the smiling girl in the photographs. He stared at the woman. He could see in her face that she wanted more from him, expected more. But it just wasn't there. "Where's your family from?" he asked.

"I'm from where you're from," she said, not without irritation. She cocked her head, and her eyes got that worried look again. "You're my father. I'm Ellen, your favorite daughter, remember?" She laughed but it sounded forced. Her voice tightened as she told him, "I'm your only child."

"My child?" he repeated and pursed his lips because he didn't think that was possible. "No, that can't be."

"Yes, it can." The skin between her eyebrows pleated. "Why do you think I keep calling you *Dad*?"

"Hmm," he said, not sure of the answer.

Her mouth came open, like she wanted to speak again, but she pursed her lips instead. Finally, she said, "All right. I need to finish fixing dinner." Then she patted his knee before getting up and walking away.

She ended up back at the sink, where she picked up an ear of corn to shuck and rinse. As the water ran, she began nattering on, about taking Sawyer into St. Louis to the Science Center for an exhibit about robots and did he want to come with them?

But Bernie didn't register the words she spoke, only the noise of her chatter, which buzzed in his head like voices at a cocktail party. He felt a shift in his awareness, and the reality of the situation hit him like a bolt of lightning. *Of course,* he thought and slapped his knees, knowing exactly where he was: at a company dinner in Coal City, his boss awarding him for a job well done.

He smiled across the way at the chattering woman with the ponytail and wondered who would take her home. He hadn't seen her arrive with anyone. Was she a secretary for one of the VPs? Bernie was sure he'd glimpsed her around the office before.

*No matter,* Bernie mused and rose to his feet. *Time*

*to work the room,* he told himself, starting toward the French doors.

"Where are you going?" the woman called to him. "Supper's almost ready, and it's a scorcher out there."

"I'm sure the caterers will ring a bell or something when it's time to eat," he said, waving a hand at her dismissively. "In the meantime, I need to find my girl. I'll bet she's outside with Jim Barbieri's wife, yakking up a storm."

"Who's Jim Barbieri?" The woman looked at him, puzzled.

Clearly she hadn't met good ol' Jim's better half yet, he thought and laughed quietly, figuring the night was still young. The pretty ponytailed gal would likely get an earful before it was over.

"Don't you worry . . . I'll take care of things." He gave her a wink, shuffling toward the doors. There he paused, glancing back. "Oh, and if you came alone to this shindig, my wife won't mind if we give you a lift home. If you haven't met Betty yet, you'll love her," he said, picturing his young bride with her teased blond hair and pink lipstick. "She's got a heart of gold."

Ellen stared at him, speechless.

Bernie grinned to himself and hobbled outside.

## Chapter 3

*Monday*

HELEN EVANS STARTED at the sound of the creaking screen door.

She wasn't expecting company.

"Hello?" she called out and quickly put aside her mop when no one answered.

Poking her head around the opened French doors that led from the cottage interior to the screened porch, she caught Amber nudging the door wide and padding inside.

*Well, for goodness' sake!*

"Where on earth have you been?" she grilled him, noticing the trail of water the cat was leaving in his wake. The green-patterned linoleum that she'd mopped only a half hour before was newly shiny with paw tracks.

He put his pink nose in the air and skulked past her.

"Oh, Amber, you know I cleaned house this morning," she said with a sigh. "Couldn't you have waited at least until tomorrow to muddy up the floor? Where'd you get such wet feet, anyhow, you old tom?" she asked as she trotted after him toward the kitchen, desperate to grab a few paper towels to wipe him off before he jumped on the furniture. "Were you after the frogs in the creek and took a dip?"

Amber's response was a stiff swish of his fat yellow tail, which looked a bit damp at the tip.

Grumbling at her four-footed charge, Helen ripped paper towels from the roll as the cat ducked his head into his food bowl and noisily began gobbling the dry nuggets.

"If you caught a frog, you didn't eat it, that's for sure," she said and squatted down beside him. "You act like you're starving to death."

Amber tried to shake away Helen's hands as she picked up his soggy left front paw and followed suit with the right, doing her best to dry him.

"I wish you'd waited until this afternoon to track in water from the creek. You're going to make me late for an engagement," she explained, chattering on as though he understood her every word. "Yes, I'm due to meet Clara at the Historical Society in ten minutes. She's twisted my arm into volunteering to sort through decades of photographs. She said that Luann Dupree has boxes and boxes of moldy pictures that no one's looked at for generations."

Amber kept eating but let out a growl low in his throat as Helen dabbed at his back feet with the paper towel.

She sighed. "Yes, I know, I'm allergic to dust, which is why I made sure to take a Claritin already. I probably should have told Clara no, but she's been acting so uncharacteristically droopy lately that I didn't have the heart to turn her down. I wonder if her arthritis is acting up again, or maybe it has to do with her brother-in-law. Word is that Bernie's Alzheimer's is getting worse by the week."

With a snort, Amber stopped eating and turned yellow eyes upon her in the fiercest glare, as if to warn, *Leave me alone if you want to keep that hand.*

"There, I'm done," Helen said and stood, her knees creaking like the old pine boards beneath her feet. She dumped the soggy towels in the trash can, shaking a finger at Amber as she scolded, "No more playing near the water, *capisce*? I'd hate to have the sheriff call someday to tell me you'd been fished out of the harbor."

Because that was where all creeks led in River Bend, Illinois: to the harbor and out to the muddy Mississippi, or was it the other way around?

*Whatever,* Helen mused, something her granddaughter would say.

The cat finished eating and stared at Helen with an unblinking gaze the color of amber, the reason Joe had chosen the moniker, even though it sounded more like a girl's name than a boy's. But Amber was the first feline her husband had agreed to let her keep in all their years of marriage. Helen wasn't about to tell Joe that he couldn't name the cat, even if she knew in her heart the old tom would be teased mercilessly by his chums. *Meow, meow, you've got a girl's name!*

Ha! She chuckled at her silly thoughts.

It was good to be able to laugh easily again. After Joe had passed suddenly three years ago from a heart attack, Helen felt for a long while like she'd forgotten how.

Amber clearly didn't share her amusement. He scowled at her like Grumpy Cat.

"What? You don't like to be nagged?" she asked him and shrugged. "Well, that's too bad. I'm your mother. I worry."

Though nary a mew escaped his pink-gummed mouth, Amber's tail shot straight up in the air and began to twitch. Then he sauntered off toward her bedroom, where he'd doubtless take a nice long post-frog-hunting nap atop the handmade quilt on her bed.

*Kids,* Helen mused with a shake of her head. Four-legged or two-footed, it didn't matter. They still didn't listen.

She grabbed the mop from where she'd leaned it against the fridge. As it was slightly damp from its earlier use, she gave the floors a quick pass. Once done, she wrung it out, set it outside to dry, and washed her hands, figuring she was good to go. Amber would likely conk out for the next few hours, so she wouldn't have to worry about anything he might track in—or drag in, for that matter—until she was home.

"I'll be back before you're awake," Helen called out as she patted the pockets of her warm-up jacket, making sure she'd tucked in cash for lunch. She planned to grab something from the diner once her session at the Historical Society was up.

She paused by the dining room mirror to give her short 'do a pat. She squinted at the grooves that dissected a face that had long ago helped earn her the title of Engineering Queen at Washington University. *Maybe a little powder,* she thought before shrugging. There wasn't much she could do with her wrinkles, despite all the potions and lotions that lined the drugstore shelves meant to fight them.

*Ah, well.* She figured it was better to look rumpled than too tight, like she'd had her face pressed with a hot iron. Besides, she'd earned every fault line on her seventy-five-year-old puss, along with the steel gray of her hair. She'd seen too many attractive older women who'd let society's ideals of staying eternally youthful turn them into caricatures of themselves.

*Better to leave things alone than tamper with perfection, eh?*

"Ha!" Helen let loose another laugh, smiling as she swiped lip balm across her mouth. Then she headed out, letting the screen door slap closed behind her.

A cardinal twittered from the oak across the street,

and she looked up as she went down her porch steps. But it wasn't the birdcall that made her stop in her tracks.

"Oh, dear," she said as she gazed across Jersey Avenue. She realized the reason for Amber's wet feet, and it had nothing to do with chasing amphibians.

The water beneath the bridge that crossed to Springfield had risen overnight and its surface bubbled like witches' brew. The swollen creek seemed ready to crest its banks. Indeed, it had breached a crack in the concrete wall at a spot near the cluster of bushes where Amber liked to stalk mice. Doubtless that was where he'd gotten those damp paws and tail. On an average day the creek babbled in a whisper. Now the noisy gurgle and swirl filled her ears as the rushing water carried twigs and leaves on its current.

Seeing no cars on the graveled road, Helen crossed toward the bridge and put her hands on the railing. From this vantage point, she could spy where the creek curved behind a clapboard cottage across the way, the waters spilling into her neighbor's backyard.

"It's rising fast and soon to crest," she said and pursed her lips, knowing that was bad news for all of River Bend and every other town within the Mississippi Valley.

It used to be that spring floods happened once every decade. In recent years they had become annual events, sometimes lasting well into summer, and it had little to do with too much rain and more to do with the increasingly wet winter weather to the north. When all that snow and ice melted upriver, it had nowhere to go but down.

Was this climate change in action? she wondered.

If it was, she didn't like it one little bit.

Should the creek continue rising at this rate, Helen would soon have to keep Amber sequestered inside the cottage. He'd have to play with toy mice instead of real ones and use his litter box and not the dirt (things he loathed and had resisted to such a degree that she'd given up on making him an indoor cat).

She figured it wouldn't be long before most of the sidewalks and roads disappeared altogether beneath the murky river water. One saving grace: her house and most all of the residences in River Bend had long ago raised their foundations, wrapping latticework to hide the piers. Any homes that hadn't been jacked up since the Great Flood of 1993 either were situated on higher ground, like those on the incline of Bluff Street, or suffered the consequences.

"How do, Helen," a raspy voice said from behind her. "Not a pretty sight, eh?"

She turned to find Agnes March, owner of the local antiques store, smiling tightly, her finely lined skin reminding Helen of crinkled parchment paper.

"Hello, Agnes," she said. "It's disheartening, isn't it?"

"It looks like we'll need a rowboat soon to get around."

"Oh, I sincerely hope not." Helen sighed.

Agnes fiddled with the pearls at her collar. "I just ran home to check on Sweetum," she said, and Helen nodded, knowing Sweetum referred to her Westie rather than a significant other, although Agnes probably considered the pooch exactly that. "I glanced out back and nearly had a panic attack. The creek had gotten high enough to swallow a pair of Adirondack chairs I had down on the lawn."

"I hope this isn't going to be another Great Flood," Helen replied.

Back in '93 she'd been afraid even her home's distance from the river and the piles that lifted it an extra three feet off the ground wouldn't be enough. At the lowest point in the valley the water had gotten as high as twenty feet. That record elevation had been marked on an old oak near the boardwalk so folks would never forget, as if they ever could. Businesses had been shuttered, houses had ended up full of mud—and fish and snakes—and anything not moved to higher ground had been lost or damaged. It was as though River Bend had drowned only to be revived and resurrected by its people, who would not give up.

But every spring when the forecasters warned of rising waters, the citizens of River Bend collectively held their breath.

"I'd better get back to the shop," Agnes said in her gritty tone. "I need to peddle what I can now, before the River Road's submerged and the tourists can't get here without wending their way into town via the back roads, which most won't take the time to do."

"I'll walk with you," Helen said, since she was heading that direction. She fell into step beside the other woman, ambling toward the downtown.

Agnes prattled on about selling a vintage tome on Native American arts and artifacts to a history buff in Alton and attending a weekend estate sale in Clifton Terrace where she'd scooped up a sixty-piece collection of Blue Willow–pattern china. Helen murmured appropriate "ohs" and "uh-huhs" while sporadically casting her gaze toward the flooded creek that twisted through River Bend. When her glances between the homes and buildings they passed revealed water spilling into the backyards, her chest clenched.

How long before it reached Main Street? A couple days? A week?

They were approaching the row of storefronts across from the diner with the Cut 'n' Curl, the sheriff's office, and Agnes's antiques store, when Agnes grabbed Helen's arm and stopped.

"I think I'll detour and grab a coffee at the diner before I get back to work," she said, her dark eyes focused on a pair of women standing in front of the Historical Society building about a block up.

Helen spotted her dear friend Clara Foley, a heavyset woman with a fondness for floral muumuus, in the thick of conversation with lanky Sarah Biddle, the sheriff's wife. Sarah was a good twenty years younger than Helen and Clara, but she was a decent bridge player and quite an adept conversationalist, to put it mildly. Sarah and Clara were both a part of Helen's regular Monday-night bridge crowd and were, some said, the town's biggest gossips. Clearly Agnes didn't want to risk getting drawn into a gabfest on the sidewalk.

"If you'll excuse me, Helen, I'll be off," Agnes murmured, departing with a backhanded wave.

"Yes, of course," she replied as Agnes hurried across the street.

She watched the trim figure in navy-blue dress and matching pumps make a beeline for the diner. Then Helen turned her attention back to Clara and Sarah. She gave a tug to her warm-up jacket before resuming her trek up the sidewalk, catching bits and pieces of conversation as she headed toward them.

". . . and I just can't imagine that she'd do such a thing," Sarah was saying. "It isn't like her to be so rash."

"Maybe she needed a break," Clara responded, clutching a large tote bag to her breasts. "Everyone gets the itch to run away once in a while."

"Without warning?"

"Why would she need to warn anyone? She's of age."

Helen cleared her throat. "Good morning, ladies," she said, greeting them with a tentative smile.

"Good morning," Clara said, absent any smile in return.

"I don't know about good, but it's a curious morning, anyway," Sarah piped up, frowning. Her left eye did a nervous tic. "We were chatting, Clara and I, about Luann. I didn't know if you heard that she . . ."

"Oh, yes, I heard you from a block away," Helen cut

her off, exaggerating only a bit. "Perhaps we could move the conversation inside the building so we don't take up the sidewalk?"

Clara glanced at Sarah Biddle. "If only we could, but apparently we cannot." She sighed and rolled her eyes behind her wire-rim spectacles.

Helen scrunched up her brow. "Am I missing something?"

"That's what we're debating." Clara glared at the sheriff's wife. "Are we missing something, Sarah, or did this *something* wander off on its own two legs? You said her car was gone . . ."

"Just because the Fiat's not here, doesn't mean she went of her own free will," Sarah insisted, cheeks inflamed. "For all we know, she was drugged and put in the trunk."

"In the trunk of a Fiat?" Clara's eyes widened and she let out a coarse laugh. She waggled her bulging tote before her. "I doubt you could even fit a bag of groceries in the back of that car. It's no bigger than a toy. Although I'm sure it could hold plenty of clowns."

"This isn't funny!" The sheriff's wife tightened hands to fists.

"Okay, stop this, the both of you," Helen said, stepping into the argument. She was about ready to strangle them both. "Will one of you tell me what the heck is going on?" She looked at her old friend Clara, who hugged her bag again defensively, then at the sheriff's wife, hoping one of them would spit it out.

"It's Luann," Sarah said and stuck out her chin. "I thought she'd be here—that her message was a joke—but apparently I was wrong. The door is locked, and she's not answering the bell or her phone. We can't get in. Frank thinks the mayor might have another key to the building, so he's gone off to fetch it."

"Luann isn't here?" Helen repeated, looking from one woman to the other. "What message? Did she go pick up coffee at the diner? I don't understand."

"Luann isn't at the diner. She isn't anywhere in River Bend," Sarah blurted out then hesitated. Her oversize teeth bit her lip before she finished with a breathless "Oh, Helen! It looks like Luann is gone for good!"

## Chapter 4

"Gone for good?" Helen repeated. Seeing the distress in Sarah's face, she couldn't help but ask, "Is she *dead*?"

"Dead?" Clara nearly choked on the word. Her neck wobbled as she declared, "Nothing's wrong with Luann Dupree except a midlife crisis."

"We don't know that nothing's wrong," Sarah said, seemingly on the verge of tears. "At the very least, she's taken off with a virtual stranger. At worst, she's been kidnapped and dragged off God knows where!"

"Good Lord, but you're being dramatic." Clara rolled her eyes. "You told me she sent you a text this morning. So she's clearly alive and well."

"*If* that was her," Sarah retorted, flipping back mousy brown hair. "You never know these days. She could have had her phone stolen or hacked."

"Baloney!" Clara snapped. "What she's done is run

off with a man. That's the gist of it, anyway, and you know it."

Helen had heard enough. "Run off with *what* man?" she demanded. "What the heck is going on here?"

Not that she was privy to everyone's deep, dark secrets, but Helen was pretty well versed on the comings and goings of the regulars in River Bend. Still, she hadn't realized Luann Dupree was seriously involved with anyone, and she was feeling more than a little frustrated by the piecemeal—and argumentative—way this story was unraveling.

"For heaven's sake, will one of you explain?" she said. "Is Luann in some kind of trouble?"

"You tell her, Sarah. You're the Runaway Bride's BFF," Clara said and crossed her arms, glancing impatiently at the Historical Society's front door.

*Runaway Bride?*

"Has Luann eloped?" Helen asked.

"No, I don't think so," Sarah said quickly then shrugged. "Well, at least not yet." She drew in a deep breath as she seemed to gather her thoughts. "Lu kept the relationship pretty quiet after she met him online a while back. She told me they clicked from the start and that he appreciated her and loved hearing about her work with the Historical Society. I'm not sure when it got so serious but I guess it must have."

Sarah stopped to pull her smartphone from her pocket. She began scrolling through messages on the small screen. "I got a text from her before breakfast. She must have left River Bend sometime yesterday. It doesn't make sense."

Helen nudged the bridge of her glasses up her nose before looking at the exchange Sarah pointed out.

I think I'm in love. We're going on a real
adventure. Yolo!!!

"What's Yolo?" she asked.

She wasn't big on texting, so she didn't know all the shorthand. She still preferred to talk on the phone or, better yet, face-to-face. She owned a flip phone, for goodness' sake. She didn't need anything smarter, or maybe she just didn't want a gadget that made her act dumber. She'd seen too many folks walk into walls or drive through stop signs because they couldn't put down their cellies.

"It means *you only live once*," Sarah Biddle told her and slipped her phone back in her pocket. Her shoulders slumped. "Lu had been alone for so long, and I know she liked this guy. She told me that he *got* her, that he actually listened when she discussed her work. They had their first real date in Grafton on Saturday night."

"So you hadn't met him?"

"No. She didn't even tell me his name. She just called him Mr. Maybe." Sarah shifted on her Crocs. "I even showed Lu's picture to the bartender at the Loading Dock, where she met her date, asking if he remembered her."

"Did he?"

"Yes."

Helen prodded. "What about Mr. Maybe? Did the bartender recall him?"

"Just that he looked like an average guy," Sarah replied solemnly. "Average height, average weight, and a full beard that was mostly brown with a little gray, so I'm guessing he's middle-aged."

"I hate beards," Clara mumbled.

"Doesn't give you much to go on, does it?" Helen admitted.

"Why should it matter?" Clara injected. "Who cares what Luann's mystery man looks like if he hasn't committed a crime?"

"How do we know that he hasn't?" Sarah narrowed her eyes. "Why would Lu take off on the spur of the moment with someone she'd just met in person for the first time? She's not impulsive like that."

"Could be she decided he was as close to Mr. Right as she was going to get," Clara said with a sniff. "She was impulsive enough to get involved in an online romance. What happened to being introduced to gentlemen by friends, or getting to know someone at church?" Her voice hummed with disapproval. "If Luann was that desperate, what makes you think she wouldn't go away with him, especially if she was smitten? Love makes people daft."

Helen wasn't sure whether to laugh or to wince. If Luann Dupree's impetuous decision to take off had been driven by her heart, it would hardly be surprising. Helen had done her share of silly things in the name of love.

But clearly the sheriff's wife wasn't buying it.

"I don't get the timing." Sarah continued gnawing on her lip. "Luann wouldn't have left now. She was so excited about her latest project. She mentioned finding something that could be extremely valuable in the boxes she cleared out of the attic for the renovation. She said she needed to do some research to be sure of what she had, maybe get a second opinion from an expert, but she had a gut feeling it was authentic—"

"Extremely valuable?" Clara interrupted with a snort. "I'll bet she found another carton of musty old pictures, as if there aren't enough of them to sort through already."

"You're not taking this seriously," Sarah scolded.

"And you're taking this way *too* seriously," Clara retorted. "I'd wager your suspicious nature is a side effect of being wed to law enforcement, or else you're watching too many crime shows on TV."

"Now, now, Clara," Helen said quietly. "You can't blame Sarah for being concerned about a friend."

"I have enough family troubles to worry about without wasting a moment fretting over Luann Dupree," Clara replied. "She's a grown woman. If she decided to ditch this tiny town to rendezvous with her lover, then, I say, good for her. Life is too short, and sometimes even when it's long it's no fairy tale."

Helen stared at Clara, hearing the pain in her voice as clearly as she saw it in her face. Yes, Clara had been cranky lately and not her usual vivacious self. But this went beyond "having a bad day." Something was clearly not right with her. Helen aimed to find out what it was once they had some privacy, not while they were standing on the street, fretting over Luann Dupree.

"You don't have to be snarky," the sheriff's wife said with a frown.

Clara scowled.

"Can't we all just get along?" Helen said and looked beseechingly at both women. "We could go grab some coffee and a doughnut at the diner and wait there until the sheriff turns up with a key . . ."

As if on cue, a male voice called out, "Hey, ladies! I got it!"

Helen glanced past Sarah to see Sheriff Biddle huffing and puffing toward them. He shook a silver key ring in his raised fist.

"It's not the key to the city," he announced, once he'd caught his breath. "But it'll get us into the Historical Society, piece of cake."

The sheriff's wife looked fit to pop. "You took long enough," she groused before snatching the key from his hand.

While he blushed sheepishly and mumbled an apology about having to wake up the town's ninety-one-year-old mayor, Sarah stabbed the key in the lock and pushed open the door.

"Hey, honey bun, maybe I should go in first, just in case," Sheriff Biddle was saying, though his wife ignored him and rushed inside.

Helen watched Sarah head up the staircase, calling out, "Luann? Lu, are you here?" while she, Clara, and the sheriff entered into the building behind her.

For a moment the three stood in the anteroom and said nothing, cocking heads, listening to Sarah's footsteps on the creaky floors above, the only noise interrupting the quiet.

"Um, should we be looking for something?" Helen asked, rubbing palms on the sides of her warm-up pants.

"Are you buying into Sarah's paranoia?" Clara muttered. "You think we'll find a trail of blood?" She clicked tongue against teeth. "More like we'll find skid marks, the woman took off so quickly with her Internet Romeo. Otherwise, what did she have to look forward to but a life of spinsterhood with lots of crusty old relics to keep her company?"

*Does anyone even use the word* spinster *anymore?* Helen wondered.

"Sarah was right. You *are* being snarky. Care to tell me what's up?"

Clara looked at her and opened her mouth, as if to explain, but the sheriff interrupted.

"Why don't you gals stay put for a minute," he said, tipping his hat back on his forehead. "I'll be right back," he told them before he went around switching on ceiling lights and illuminating artifact-filled glass cases. He ambled up the hallway, disappearing into one room and then another, shouting over his shoulder, "All clear," each time he emerged, until he'd hit them all.

"Did you find anything out of order?" Helen asked when he returned.

"There's nothing besides a puddle of water in the back room. It's coming in beneath the door," he said and rubbed his bulldog-like jowls. "The creek's pretty high already. As attached as Ms. Dupree is to this Historical Society, it does seem odd that she'd leave town without sandbagging first, although Sarah said she must have left in a hurry."

"Hmm," Helen murmured. She tended to agree with him, knowing how Luann had championed funding for the building and its renovation the past ten years. Would she run off with a man and leave all her prized relics at the mercy of the rising floodwaters?

"What I find odd," Clara argued, "is that we're standing around debating the actions of an adult female whose brain is most certainly muddled by hormones. C'mon, Helen," she said and gave Helen's arm a tug. "Let's get to work going through those photographs. They're not going to sort themselves."

Helen glanced at the sheriff, who shrugged. "I don't know any reason you folks can't do your volunteer work. I'll go check on Sarah," he added and hitched up his khaki pants, which, despite the belt, sagged below his oversized belly.

Before he'd gone halfway up, Sarah appeared, stairs creaking as she made her way down. She held something in her hand. Whatever it was, she looked relieved.

The sheriff said nothing until they'd both reached the ground floor.

"What did you find?" he asked as his wife wriggled an object in his face.

Helen noticed it was a small and very slim dark blue book.

"It's her passport," Sarah replied breathlessly. "If she left it behind, she can't mean to travel too far, right? Her suitcase is gone and some clothes were strewn about like she packed quickly." She paused to remark, "I picked them up, of course. I'd hate for things to be a mess when she got back. Surely she won't be gone for long."

"So I was right." Clara harrumphed. "She did go looking for Mr. Goodbar, or traveling with Mr. Goodbar, anyway."

"Stop it," Helen said under her breath, nudging her friend as Sarah Biddle gave Clara the stink eye.

The sheriff patted his wife's back. "Yep, I'll bet she's back soon enough. Try not to worry," he advised, though Sarah merely bit her lower lip, looking a little like a frightened bunny. "How about we go and leave Mrs. Evans and Mrs. Foley to their volunteer work, unless you'd like to stay and help them?"

Before Sarah could open her mouth to reply, Clara raised a hand, like a traffic cop making a stop in the middle of the street.

"No, no! You go on," she directed. "I know exactly what to do. Thanks for letting us in, Sheriff. We would have been sitting on the curb otherwise."

He tipped his hat at her then turned to Helen. "Would you lock up when you leave, ma'am? Then could you come by to drop off the spare?" he asked, handing over the key ring he'd obtained from the mayor. "I'd like to keep those in my desk until Ms. Dupree returns."

"Will do, Sheriff," she told him, taking the keys and pocketing them. They made a good-sized lump in her warm-up jacket but didn't appear at risk for falling out.

"Thank you," he said. "Now I think I'd best talk to the town council about getting some volunteers to sandbag out back. We've got to get a serious effort going now. Don't want the water to catch us unawares. Ma'am," he added, touching his cap as he nodded at Helen and Clara.

When the town's sole law enforcement officer guided his wife out the front door, Clara let loose a big sigh.

"Thank goodness that's over. How about we go upstairs?" Clara suggested, hefting her tote bag onto her shoulder. "Luann has a table set up in the storage area. That was easier for her than moving all the boxes downstairs. We've wasted enough time as it is squabbling over that silly woman's whereabouts. I always thought she was a bit daffy."

Helen wasn't sure what to say to that. She'd had only brief conversations with Luann Dupree at various town functions, mostly along the lines of "How are you? Nice weather we're having, isn't it?" She had attended several of Luann's town hall lectures about the Mississippi River Valley, the roots of their tiny village, local legends like the Piasa Bird, and the possibility of Lewis and Clark setting foot in River Bend. But Helen didn't know her well, not personally, and she hadn't been volunteering at the Historical Society for years, like Clara. She had found Luann very credible and hardly daffy when it came to her work, anyway. But she'd known plenty of folks with lots of brains and little common sense. Maybe that was the case with Luann.

As Clara had remarked, love did seem to alter one's brain chemistry. Even those with a good head on their shoulders could lose it when their hearts got in the way, she decided as they climbed the steps to the second-floor landing.

"Don't get distracted by what's around us," Clara said, ushering Helen into a vast room with big windows. "It's a bit like stumbling upon the greatest garage sale you've ever seen. Only nothing has a price tag and, according to Luann, everything is priceless."

Even before Clara hit the light switch, Helen could see what she was talking about.

While the area was mostly devoid of furniture—save for a dozen card tables and chairs—there were plenty of boxes. They were piled high on one side of the room. On the other there were more boxes, these opened, with contents lined up on card tables set in a row. Helen wandered nearer to see pieces of regional pottery, old glass bottles, even a handmade purple two-headed doll with lace hair.

"This all belongs to the Historical Society?" she found herself asking. It looked like someone had robbed all the guests on a season's worth of *Antiques Roadshows*.

"What you see downstairs in the cases is just a fraction of the collection," Clara told her. "There isn't room to show off everything. Luann found dozens of moving boxes left behind by the previous director that had never been opened. I told her she needed to bring in some help, like *real* help, someone who knows what these things are worth, maybe the curator from a museum. But she said she didn't want anyone else poking around *her* things. She was afraid they'd steal pieces from under her nose."

Helen thought of what Sarah Biddle had said, about Luann finding something valuable, though she couldn't imagine who'd want to steal pottery or a two-headed doll. But what did she know? Oh, sure, she could tell a Queen Anne chair from a Windsor, but she was hardly an expert in antiquities.

"Perhaps Agnes could assist her? Everyone trusts Agnes."

"If Luann discussed priceless relics with anyone, I'd hardly be the wiser. She most definitely did not share her secrets with me." Clara wiggled an arm at a particular table loaded with rubber-banded stacks of photos. "Now, let's get going on the sorting, or we'll be here all day and all night just to get through this latest batch."

Helen did as advised, picking one of the cushioned folding chairs on either side of the table that Clara had indicated. Clara pulled a particular stack her way and pushed another toward Helen.

"Those are from about twenty years back," Clara told her. "So you and Joe would have lived here for thirty years by then. See if you recognize anyone or anything. Separate the photos of folks you can identify and write a name or location on the back with acid-free ink. Then place it in this green bin," Clara said, pointing to a plastic cubby to Helen's right. "If you don't see anyone or any particular place that resonates, place it in the red bin." That one was to Helen's left.

"Got it," she said. "What's in your pile, might I ask?"

"Since I was born in River Bend, Luann has me going through photos dating back sixty years or more." She shook her head. "It's a revelation, let me tell you. Some of them take my breath away, reminding me of moments I'd forgotten." Again, sadness crept into her face.

Helen took the opportunity to say, "What's going on with you, hon? Something isn't right. I can tell."

Her old friend hesitated, pursing her lips. The distressed expression was suddenly replaced by anger.

"Dang it, Helen, I know you've probably heard that Bernie's not well, but it's worse than that," she finally admitted, referring to her brother-in-law. "Poor Betty is at wit's end. I know it's death to the person going through Alzheimer's. I do understand that. I can't even imagine watching my mind slip away. But it's murder for the caretaker and the family, too. It breaks my heart to pieces, particularly when Bernie says something hurtful to Betty or Ellen. Even if he doesn't mean to . . ."

Clara choked up and couldn't finish.

Helen reached for her hand, seeing the tears in her eyes. "I'm sorry," she whispered. "I wish there was something I could to do help."

"I know," Clara said and sniffled. "But it seems like now it's just a waiting game, and not a very pleasant one at that." She slipped her hand away from Helen's and wiped away her tears. "Good Lord, I hate being maudlin," she said and quickly patted her gray pin curls. "That's why I like having work to do. So let's try to get something done around here, even if the Society's director has snubbed us to gallivant about with a mystery man."

Helen hoped that was actually the case and Sarah Biddle's fears weren't warranted.

"Oh, I did bring us something to nibble when we need a break."

Helen smiled. Her friend had always had a taste for sweets. But then, who didn't, she thought and smoothed a hand over her own lumpy belly.

"When I worry, I bake." Clara reached into her tote bag to pull out a Ziploc bag filled with muffins. "Banana chocolate chip," she said, "made fresh this morning."

There was still steam clinging to the inside of the

baggie. Helen nearly swooned when Clara opened it up and the aroma of muffins filled the air.

"Do we really have to wait?" Helen asked.

Clara chuckled. "What the heck! Let's have one now. It'll give us more energy, won't it?"

"Oh, it certainly will."

Helen chuckled as her friend unearthed napkins from her bag and then doled out a treat for each. "A muffin a day keeps the doctor away. Isn't that how it goes?"

"If it doesn't, it should!"

Now, *this* was the Clara she knew and loved, Helen thought, glad to see the old Clara back for now. They fell into an amiable silence as they nibbled on the muffins and began sorting through the dozens of black-and-white photographs from River Bend's past.

## Chapter 5

JACKSON LEE SAT in his car, parked catty-corner from the two-story Victorian house with the wraparound porch.

He feigned talking on his phone, gesticulating as though he were in a heated discussion, when an occasional car or dog walker passed. The trick to stalking a client was acting like he wasn't paying attention to anything at all. If someone had knocked on the glass and asked what he was doing, Jackson would have pointed to his phone and said, "Trying to figure out how I got so darned lost."

It worked every time.

But no one had disturbed him in the ten minutes he'd been patiently waiting. He checked the clock on his phone, figuring he didn't have much longer to go.

Still, it was frustrating, not being able to just head

up the paver path, knock on the door, and say, "Hey, Bernie, remember me? I've got the deal of a lifetime that you'll want to get in on before it's too late."

He just needed to get the old man to scribble on the dotted line, no matter how illegible, then Jackson could grab a check—signed or not, so long as it had the bank account and routing numbers, it was good as gold—and then the deal would be done.

With a sigh, he squinted through his Ray-Bans at the Victorian, giving it a critical once-over. The peeling clapboards could have used a new coat of paint and the overgrown grass a good mowing, but he ventured to guess the place was worth a bundle, even if it needed a bit of sprucing up. He'd done business with enough of the senior citizens who populated River Bend to understand that the town was a gold mine for guys like him: hungry independent contractors well versed in fiscal seduction. Jackson had a background in the theater and knew how to play to his audience. It didn't hurt that he had a great head of hair, perfect teeth, and blue eyes that could charm the pants off any heterosexual woman with a pulse, something he'd done a time or ten, which was probably why he'd never married. Romance could be very profitable, particularly if he found the right mark, and he had, more often than not.

"You remind me of someone, hon," Erma, his regular waitress at the diner, had said to him the other morning. "Oh, I know!" Her rumpled face had lit up. "Who's that Irish actor that played James Bond?"

"Do you mean Pierce Brosnan?" Jackson had replied, because he'd heard that comparison often enough. He'd puffed out his chest and tugged at the knot of his silk tie—yes, he still dressed for work, a lost art in a world ruled by Casual Fridays.

Erma had pursed her lips, thinking for a moment. "No, that's not who I'm talking about. You know, it's the fellow that was only in one movie before they canned him."

Jackson had sighed. "Timothy Dalton?"

"Nope."

"George Lazenby?"

The woman had brightened up instantly. "Yep! That's him!"

"He was Australian," Jackson told her. "Not Irish."

"Really?" Erma's penciled-in eyebrows arched. "I guess I just get confused by the accents. They're tricky sometimes," she remarked in her flat Midwestern drawl.

"Oh, yes, so tricky," he had said and smiled tolerantly, thinking the Lazenby comparison didn't bode well for the day ahead, did it?

If there was one thing he wasn't, Jackson mused, it was a one-hit wonder.

No salesman worth his salt could survive unless he kept getting hit after hit. If there were an award for success in this game—beyond a score—he surely would have won it.

So he tried to put Erma's comment out of his head,

focusing on the house and what had brought him here on this fine afternoon.

He was well acquainted with the owner: Bernie Winston was his name. Jackson had done business with Bernie several times in the past. The old guy had shown up like clockwork every Sunday morning at the Jerseyville Country Club to play a round of golf with a quartet of gray-hairs who had all been willing targets. Jackson liked to hit them up at the coffee shop, when they were hanging out after banging that little white ball around for hours, blessedly free of their nosy wives.

He appreciated Bernie for what he was: a frustrated retiree who'd been forced out of a career he'd loved and hadn't known what to do with himself when it was gone. He was exactly the type of man who was Jackson's bread and butter. They needed to feel important, particularly after they'd lost the one thing that made them feel like they truly mattered: their job title. Jackson knew all the right words to say. He usually warmed them up with a slap on the back and a little brownnosing along the lines of "It's clear that you've got smarts in spades. I'll bet you recognize a good thing when you see it."

Then Jackson would ease into a soft sell of whatever investment he was pitching: an East Texas oil well, a condo complex in the Ozarks, or a stake in a commercial property, say, a new restaurant in downtown Alton. He'd act like it was the best thing since sliced bread but also untenable. "Oh, man, I wish I could get you in on it, but I think every share is sold out."

Then, of course, they'd insist on getting in. Jackson made them feel like it was their idea to give him money, not his. He made sure they got a little profit by robbing Peter to pay Paul, which guaranteed they'd want in the next time, figuring they'd make even more.

When last he'd encountered Bernie, he'd hooked him on a parcel of land for sale downriver. He told good old Bern that there was interest from a casino (but what he hadn't shared was that the land had some kind of environmental contamination). Bernie had gone for that one like a hot potato.

He hadn't heard from Bernie in a while, a long while. So he'd asked around at the club this past week, and he'd been told Bernie's brain had been slip-sliding away. "Poor guy doesn't know if he's coming or going," a former golfing pal had said with a shake of his head.

But Jackson didn't pity him. He didn't pity anyone.

What he believed in, beyond the almighty dollar, was Darwin's theory of survival of the fittest. Some folks thrived, while others withered. If you were a frail little mouse, you were apt to be eaten by a mighty hawk, right? That was just how it went, the ubiquitous circle of life.

Jackson's first thought at learning Bernie Winston had gone daft was nothing short of gratitude. Because if he'd reeled Bernie in when he had some of his marbles, imagine what he could do with a marbleless Bernie!

Yep, old Bern was the perfect patsy.

Jackson had another pitch lined up: an investment in an old flour mill on the riverfront targeted for renovation into elegant lofts. He had a contract ready, tucked in his inside pocket.

Now, if only Bernie's wife would take off in her gray Chevy Malibu, which she usually did around this time every Monday at lunchtime. She left Bernie at home all by his lonesome and headed out on the River Road into Alton to do her weekly grocery shopping. Jackson had drunk a lot of coffee at the diner in weeks past, planning for his conquest, mostly while he'd gathered intel via eavesdropping and from an unsuspecting Erma. He'd also put in some time doing drive-by surveillance to confirm the facts.

He was nothing if not thorough.

A low noise rent the air, like the faraway rumble of a jet.

Jackson shifted in his seat, watching as the garage door rolled up and the gray sedan backed out. He ducked his head, putting his phone up to his left ear as the car's back end bumped into the street. Tires popping over gravel, the Malibu shifted into Drive and headed away, kicking up dust in its tracks.

"It's about time," he grumbled.

He took one last look at himself in the mirror. After smoothing a hand over the sticky pomade in his hair, he winked.

"You've still got it, Jackson Lee," he said, giving himself a pep talk. "Now go get 'em!"

He popped open the door of his beloved DeVille, sidled out onto the street, and sauntered toward the Victorian's brick-paved path. When he reached the front porch, he buttoned his blazer, clearing his throat before he laid a few sound knocks on the door.

"You there, Bernie, old friend?" he called out, peering through the panes of glass on either side of the threshold. "It's me, your buddy Jackson Lee!"

He knew there was the possibility that Bernie wouldn't come to the door. Heck, the old guy might not even know how to unlock it. Jack had heard that the missus had taken away Bernie's car keys, and he'd had a feeling the same thing had happened to Bernie's cell phone, which Jackson had futilely tried calling in the recent past. He just hoped old Bern still kept his checkbook in that painted secretary in the living room.

Jackson *knew* if he could get to Bernie without a woman in the way, he'd find exactly what he needed. It didn't even matter if Bernie was only semilucid or even delusional. If he could hold a pen, he could make his mark on the contract. Then he could stand aside while Jackson located a blank check and forget that he ever saw him, which was pretty much guaranteed.

It sounded so easy.

"Hey, Bern, open up!" After another round of fist pounding and a few leans on the doorbell, sure enough, Jackson spied his target ambling toward him.

He heard some fumbling that lasted far too long

before the door swung inward, and Jackson found himself facing Bernie Winston in the flesh.

"Hey, bud, how're you doing?" he said and slapped him companionably on the shoulder, while Bernie blinked at him, clearly trying to size him up. "You're looking good for a guy who hasn't hit the golf course in a coon's age."

Which was a total lie.

Bernie didn't look good at all. He looked stoop-shouldered and wild-eyed. His skin had a vaguely ashy tone and was mottled with brown spots. His white hair seemed sparser than ever and showed plenty of his pale, freckled scalp.

But Jackson didn't let on his shock. That was where his acting chops came in handy.

"Do I know you?" Bernie asked, standing dumbly before him like a roadblock. "Are you with Human Resources?"

"Oh, it's better than that. We're business partners," Jackson said, trying to nudge the old man aside so he could enter and shut the door behind them. He didn't want any neighbors spying him at the door and thinking something was wrong.

"We're business partners," Bernie repeated.

"Yep, I'm going to help you get rich, pal, and you're lucky I came today 'cause I've got the hottest ticket in town. It's an old mill on the river, and it's ripe for development—"

"A mill?" Bernie interrupted. "Are you with Peabody?" His caterpillar-white eyebrows knitted. "We only deal in mines."

"You're right. It's a coal mine. Silly me! How about we go inside and talk about it." Jackson finally managed to get past the old coot, sidling into the living room.

There were signs tacked everywhere—big, bold, black letters written on white paper stuck to various items. On the phone: *Don't answer!* Above the thermostat: *Don't touch!* On the back of the door: *Don't let anyone in!*

Thank goodness Bernie had ignored the latter, or maybe he couldn't read too well anymore.

"Do I know you?" the old man asked again, coming up behind him.

So Jackson went through the whole rigmarole all over again. "It's me, Jackson Lee. I'm your pal. We go way back. I've got an investment for you that you won't want to miss."

"We're pals?"

"Yes, sir, from way back." Jackson unbuttoned his jacket and reached for the paperwork he'd brought with him. "Don't worry about finding a pen. I've got one!" He plucked his lucky Cartier Roadster ballpoint from his breast pocket—lucky 'cause he'd won it off his car-dealer buddy in last week's poker game—and he tapped the final page of the contract he'd laid out on the sofa table. "I just need your John Hancock right here, my friend. And if you'll allow me to locate your checkbook, I'll handle the transaction without you having to lift a finger . . ."

"Did you say you were from Peabody?" Bernie interrupted, shuffling toward him. "Am I getting a raise?"

"Oh, yeah," Jackson told him, motioning him nearer, "a big one. All you have to do is sign right here, then let's find your checkbook, and we'll get squared away."

He pushed the pen into Bernie's right hand. He saw the old man's fingers tremble as he fiddled with it, turning it around and around before he seemed to recall how to hold it properly.

"Your signature, my friend, that's all that's standing in the way between you and your windfall."

Jackson held his breath as Bernie touched the ball-point to the paper. His shaky hand jerked, starting a wiggly line that looked vaguely more legible through a squint.

"That's it . . . That's great," Jackson cooed as he headed toward the tall secretary painted with lotus blossoms or something vaguely Asian in origin. He reached for the lid over the desk and pulled it wide. He spied a red box that surely contained the checks he was looking for, only to stop cold at the sound of a voice from behind him.

"What in God's name is going on here?"

The voice wasn't Bernie's.

Jackson swiveled about, dropping the desk lid with a clatter.

Bernie dropped the pen, as well. It hit the floor and rolled under the couch.

"Well, howdy do, ma'am," Jackson said, a little rattled. He hadn't heard anyone come in, but sure enough, there she stood, glowering in the doorway. She had cotton-white hair, a sharp nose, a pointed chin, and deep grooves around her eyes and mouth. Not a woman he'd choose to cozy up to even if he were on his last dime.

"Who are you?" she snapped as Jackson took a few quick steps and snatched the papers from the coffee table.

"Well, hey, ma'am, I'm Jackson Lee, a friend of Bernie's from the country club," he drawled, acting as unaffected as he could while quickly stuffing the pages in his coat pocket. "And just who are *you*?"

As if he didn't know.

"I'm Bernie's wife," she told him, her cheeks a vivid red. "And if I hadn't forgotten my grocery list and come home to find the front door open, you would have probably gotten away with whatever you're trying to get away with!"

"I'm getting a raise," Bernie piped up, grinning crookedly. "Is that great, Betts? I have to sign some papers before it's a done deal. Then maybe we can buy that Bel Air convertible I've had my eye on."

"He's not here to give you a raise," the wife said. "He's here to steal from a senile old man." She had her cell phone in hand, and she threatened, "If you're not out of here in five seconds flat, I'm calling the sheriff . . ."

*Hell and damnation!* He'd have to come back to get that check.

"Must go. I'm late for a meeting," Jackson said then took off like a shot.

He was out the door and inside his Caddy in record time. As soon as the engine caught, he peeled out of there and didn't look back.

## Chapter 6

IT SEEMED LIKE the water had risen even in the few hours that Helen had helped Clara at the Historical Society. They had managed to sort through a whole white banker's box full of photographs, although that was merely the tip of the iceberg.

"It'll take months, if not years, to check all of them," she'd groaned, and Clara hadn't disagreed. But her friend had hardly acted discouraged. Clara had seemed very intent while looking through her batch, almost as if she was searching for something in particular or, perhaps, for someone? Clara had grown up in River Bend, as had generations before her. So it stood to reason that some of those photographs pictured her and her family.

Well, she was glad if Clara was getting something personal out of the volunteer gig. All Helen had gotten was a vague headache from squinting through her specs.

At the diner, where she and Clara had gone after their shift was done, Helen noticed tall and lanky Art Beaner, husband to Bertha and head of the town council, busy spreading word that boats needed moving from the harbor.

"Get 'em out now while you can or you're risking damage," she overheard him telling table after table. "The harbor's already so high it's a foot shy of spilling onto the parking lot."

Helen was glad that she didn't have a boat to fret about, not since Joe had been alive. She only had to worry about herself and Amber.

"Hello, Mrs. Evans, Mrs. Foley," Beaner said when he stopped by the booth where Helen sat with Clara.

"So things are looking bleak?" Helen dared to ask.

He doffed his ball cap and rubbed a hand over thinning hair. "The softball field's swamped. We've had to cancel the opening games and delay filling up the community pool. It's still drained from winter, thank heavens, but it already has a foot of muck at the bottom. Word is the river hasn't crested yet, so we're gearing up for the worst. It's only a matter of time before the harbor covers the lot and the street, threatening the homes on Harbor Drive. When that happens, we'll have to shut down the ramp into town from the River Road . . . Well, the flood will close it even if we don't."

"I'll hope for the best," Helen said, though it didn't sound good.

Art tugged back on his ball cap, squinting past them

out the plateglass window. "Looks like Biddle's getting a bagging crew together. I'd better go offer my services."

"Of course."

"Afternoon, ladies."

Helen turned toward the window as Art left them, glimpsing the sheriff closing the tailgate on a pickup truck piled high with a mountain of sand, and she wished she weren't seventy-five with arthritis and bad knees. She would have left the diner right then with Mr. Beaner, eager to lend a hand.

"I guess we can't do anything now but sit tight," she said as she faced Clara again, only to find her friend dabbing at tears in her eyes. "Oh, no, did I say something wrong? Is it the flood?"

"No, it's not. And don't look at me like that," Clara scolded. "It's the pollen count, nothing more."

"You didn't sneeze or rub your eyes at the Historical Society, and those photographs reek of must," Helen said. "Can't you tell me what's bothering you? It's Bernie, yes? Or is there something else going on?"

"It's nothing," Clara murmured. "It's my allergies."

But Helen knew that was a lie.

"We've been friends for too long for you to keep secrets from me."

Clara stopped sniffling. "Secrets," she said, "are poison."

"I'm listening."

That seemed to do the trick, as the floodgates quickly opened.

"Oh, Lord, I don't even know what to do at this point. It's just more of the same," Clara said with a sob. "Betty's at her wit's end. Caring for Bernie is really taking its toll. She's got to watch him like a baby, and he isn't letting her sleep. He wakes up at night and wanders. The other night he started swinging around a candelabra, hollering about keeping a car away that was trying to hit him. If that's not enough, she's finding misfiled paperwork dealing with their taxes, and even canceled checks for various business investments that were nothing more than scams. Sometimes I think it'd be better if he were—" She cut herself off, shaking her head. "It's just hard, you know."

"What can I do?" she asked, feeling as helpless about the situation as she did about the rising floodwaters.

Clara sighed. "I don't know what to do myself. I sit with him sometimes when she needs a break. I want her to spend time with Ellen and Sawyer without having to worry. But I can't be there every minute."

"No, you can't."

"She's finding more things that he screwed up in the past few years, paperwork for loans, checks he'd written to people she doesn't know, missed insurance payments." Clara paused and bit her lip. "It's a good thing she took away his car keys, or he might have killed someone by now. She's scared, Helen, though I don't know what she's more afraid of, the mess he's leaving her or being without him."

Helen took her hand and squeezed, all the while

thinking she had to do something more. She would talk to the girls at bridge tonight and sign them up to bake casseroles and cakes so Betty wouldn't have to worry about dinner for a few nights at least.

She remembered when Joe had his first heart attack, and the emotional and physical toll it had taken on her while she'd nursed him back to health. But that wasn't the same as caring for someone with Alzheimer's. It wasn't like those folks ever got better, only worse.

"I wish I could attend bridge tonight, but I can't," Clara said, and Helen made a noise of distress. "I told Betty I'd come over and sit with Bernie so she can go out for ice cream with Ellen and Sawyer."

"I understand."

Clara picked at her Cobb salad, the light in her blue eyes gone, and Helen did the same with her tuna sandwich. She didn't have much of an appetite herself, between talk of Bernie's condition and the Mississippi River creeping into town like an unwanted guest.

When Erma approached to elaborate on the fresh pies for dessert, Clara shook her head. Helen declined, as well, and—despite Clara's protests—asked for the check.

"Know that I'm always around if you need me," she told her friend, though she wished she could offer more than words.

"What would I do without you?" Clara said, and they shared a brief hug on the sidewalk before they parted ways.

Her heart heavy, Helen turned to look across the street at the sheriff's office.

The truck full of sand had disappeared, as had the half-dozen folks who'd been standing around it. She figured they were busy sandbagging behind the homes and businesses closer to the harbor, where the water always seemed to do the most damage. When the soft-ball field went under and the harbor waters rose, the main path into town from the River Road disappeared beneath the murky brown. As Agnes had remarked earlier, once that happened, the only way in or out was through the back roads, or else by canoe.

After the River Road closed, it was just a matter of time before the overflowing creeks that wound through River Bend began to reach the houses perched along their borders, like Agnes's residence on Springfield. Maybe the forecasters would be wrong and the water would subside before it caused too much damage.

But, Helen knew, for that to happen, they'd have to get lucky.

She waited for a car to pass then crossed Main Street and headed for the sheriff's office. He wouldn't be there, of course, but Helen could surely drop off the keys to the Historical Society and leave them on his desk with a note.

But when she entered and closed the door behind her, she saw that the chair behind the sheriff's desk was occupied. Though it wasn't Biddle who sat there; it was his wife.

"Why, hello, Sarah," she said and walked toward her.

"Are you filling in for Frank while he leads the sandbag brigade?" she asked in jest. But the sheriff's wife didn't look amused.

"Just doing a bit of research," she said, glancing up nervously from the computer. She tried to cover up something on her right—a little blue "book"—but Helen saw it and knew what it was immediately.

"Is that Luann's passport?"

Sarah Biddle opened her mouth—to lie, Helen thought—then ended up sighing. "I know you probably think I'm going overboard, like Clara does. But I can't help it. I've tried calling Lu half a dozen times. It all goes to voice mail. Instead I get text messages in response, telling me she's fine, to let her enjoy herself. But why won't she call me back so I can hear her voice?"

"Maybe she doesn't want to talk to you," Helen said, hoping she didn't hurt Sarah's feelings. "Maybe she's afraid you'll tell her she's being stupid and she'll feel like a fool."

"Well, she is being stupid!" Sarah blushed. "Oh, I see what you mean."

"Have you asked Frank to help? I always see them pinging someone's phone on TV cop shows. At least then you'd know where she was."

Sarah pulled a face. "I already asked about that. He'd have to get a warrant, only he said no judge would give him that when he doesn't have a shred of evidence that anything is wrong."

"That does make sense."

"He claims he can't even put out a be-on-the-lookout for her car, that it would divert attention from known criminal activity."

"That makes sense, too."

"He assured me there's nothing he can do, at least not until Luann asks for help or there's evidence that she's really in danger," Sarah said and appeared so distraught that Helen felt the need to say something more.

She leaned her hands on the heavy desk, looking Sarah in the eye. "I met my husband at Washington University in St. Louis back when it was a trolley-car school," she said. "He was a devil, but there was something about him I couldn't dismiss. He was charming and funny, though I'd heard rumors about his wild behavior. He drank bathtub gin in his fraternity and was temporarily blinded."

"But Joe was a teetotaler," Sarah said in disbelief, and Helen nodded.

"He became one." She laughed. "He was a dickens, all right. My girlfriends warned me about him. They said he'd been kicked out of six schools before college, and I later found out it was true." She smiled despite herself. "I had known him exactly three months when he asked me to marry him. We decided to elope and got in the car, heading for New York City, which we thought would be romantic."

"I didn't realize you and Joe eloped," Sarah remarked.

Helen laughed. "We didn't. I chickened out, so he

turned the car around and came home. It would have killed my mother if I hadn't let her plan my wedding."

"You're trying to say Lu might come to her senses."

"I'm saying that she has to make her own choices. It's her life."

Sarah didn't look reassured. "I'm not convinced she went freely. What if he took her? He could have used that date-rape drug, or pulled a gun on her. It happens, you know, even to middle-aged women."

"Do you want my advice?"

"Yes, please."

"Follow your gut and do what you need to do until you're convinced she's all right. I'm a firm believer in intuition."

"I will." Sarah gave her a half-hearted smile.

Helen turned to leave then stopped. She'd almost forgotten what she'd gone to the sheriff's office for.

Reaching into her jacket pocket, she withdrew the silver key ring Sheriff Biddle had given her earlier. "For the Historical Society," she said and returned to set them on the desk.

Sarah palmed the keys. "I'll make sure he gets them," she said before she opened the top desk drawer and dropped them in.

Helen nodded.

"Oh, by the way," Sarah called out when Helen opened the door to leave, "I can't make bridge tonight. I promised Frank I'd take dinner to the sandbaggers so they can keep working. Hope I don't leave you in a bind."

Helen waved and told her, "No worries. It's only cards."

Although walking back to her cottage, she was worrying plenty. Even since morning, the creek had swollen further, its banks no longer even pretending to contain it. Water spilled onto lawns and even into the street in spots.

Everyone she passed wore an anxious expression.

She found three messages on her voice mail from Bebe Horn, Lola Mueller, and Bertha Beaner, all canceling out on bridge that evening.

All told, that made five who'd be no-shows. So Helen called the rest and postponed indefinitely, to resume "whenever the river retreats."

To calm her nerves, she decided to sit down with the Sunday crossword, which she hadn't had time to complete yesterday, so it was only half-done.

She settled in the wicker settee on the porch, setting the folded newsprint in her lap. Amber jumped up on its arm and padded across the newspaper, finally perching on the top of the cushion beside her.

"Are you comfy?" she asked him, waiting for his yellow eyes to blink before smoothing the crossword puzzle and picking up her purple pen. "All right, let's begin. It's known as the Dza Chu in Tibet," she said, reading aloud the first clue. "It's six letters, if that helps," she added and looked at Amber.

He yawned then lifted a paw and started licking.

Helen tapped the pen to her chin, thinking she knew

it. Her granddaughter Melissa had spent a year in Asia teaching English to children and had plastered her Facebook page with countless photos and descriptions of all the places she'd seen when she'd been traveling.

"A-ha! It's *Mekong*," Helen announced abruptly, causing Amber to jerk.

She filled that one in and proceeded to another.

"He isn't what he seems," she said, "eight letters."

Amber tucked his head atop his paws and closed his eyes.

"How about *swindler*," she tried, but it didn't quite work. "*Imitator?*" she suggested. Only that wasn't right either. She tapped the purple ink to the page before another answer formed in her mind. "*Impostor,*" she said, smiling as she printed the missing letters into the tiny squares.

"God help me if my brain ever starts to rot," she remarked, giving Amber a pat.

Once she'd finished the rest of the crossword, she moved on to the jigsaw puzzle that Fanny Melville had given her as a birthday gift last month: a five-hundred-piece mosaic of colorful birds and a snowy birdhouse. She began with the border, of course, and clustered like-colored pieces together within the frame. She worked for hours with nary a break, stopping only to get up and turn on the overhead lamp as the daylight faded to dusk.

Amber took that opportunity to mew at her.

Was it dinnertime already?

She hadn't eaten since the tuna sandwich and pickles at lunch.

She thought of Clara, sitting with Bernie this evening so Betty could spend time with her daughter and granddaughter, and her heart felt heavy.

"I think I'll go keep her company," Helen said aloud, as much to herself as to Amber. "I'll take that tray of cheese and fruit I'd planned to set out for the bridge game tonight. What do you think? Good idea? Or will I be butting in?"

Amber mewed at her again, cocking his head.

"You're right." She laughed. "When have I ever cared about butting in?"

She reached for the cat, and he nipped at her fingers.

"Sorry," she told him. "Of course, I'll feed you first."

He gave her a slow blink, looking at least partially appeased, and Helen scratched him between his ears.

"How dreadful it must be to watch the person you love most deteriorate until there's not much left but the shell of them. At least I got to have my Joe until the very end. I still miss him every single day."

Amber seemed to agree. He began to purr very softly.

She sat quietly for a long moment, listening to the cat's warm rumble and hearing the loud whoosh of the creek through the screens of the porch.

The streetlamps flickered on, glistening off the wet road.

And still the water rose.

## Chapter 7

---

*Wednesday*

HELEN TUGGED ON her galoshes then hesitated as she stood. She looked around her, knowing she was forgetting something. One blurry glance at the clock, and she realized it was her bifocals.

She poked around the sofa where she'd left the morning newspaper with the crossword half-done, but she couldn't find them. Had she set them on the bedside table after dipping into the latest Carolyn Hart mystery before she'd fallen asleep last night?

Absently, she patted her head, and she realized where she'd put them.

*Oh, my.*

Her head was like the black hole for missing spectacles: every once in a while she'd find two pairs up there.

*Grandma Brain,* she thought with a laugh, because

there weren't enough puzzles in the world to keep her mind from fogging up now and then.

Amber whined at the screen door as she reached to open it, but she nudged him back with her foot. "It's too wet out there, buddy. You're going to have to stay inside. If you need to pee, your litter box is over in the corner. You know the drill."

He gave her a grumpy look and stomped off as she told him good-bye.

Then she left the house, securing the screen door so Amber couldn't pry it open with a paw. She headed to the Historical Society to help Clara go through more of the old photos for the archives. It gave her something to do beyond her crosswords, jigsaws, and quilting. She couldn't exactly work on the community garden with her cohorts in the Ladies Civic Improvement League, as the plot was currently underwater.

Pretty soon more than just the softball fields, pool, and garden would be flooded.

One glance across the street told her that the concrete walls meant to contain rising creek waters had given up entirely. Helen gauged there were at least two inches covering her own Jersey Avenue. Beyond the bridge, she could see that Springfield wasn't wet yet. But Jersey was lower and more prone to flooding. So far only the homes on Springfield with yards backing up to the creek seemed to be in any danger. Everything looked dry on the left side of that road.

But anyone departing Springfield had to drive

toward Main Street to reach the highway, also known as the Great River Road. It was the fastest and easiest way north to Grafton and Pere Marquette or south to Elsah or Alton. So unless folks took the back road out through farm country—a.k.a. the long way home—they were going to get very wet.

Still, there wasn't so much water on the sidewalks that Helen couldn't slog through the puddles from Jersey to Main Street. If she didn't look down at her boots and the twigs and sludge that swirled around them, she would have believed it was just another nice spring day.

The scenery that had looked so dull through the winter—brown trees, brown grass, bare garden plots—had suddenly greened. Buds and blossoms abounded on shrubs and branches. Birds tweeted merrily and darted about, picking up bits and pieces to build nests. As always happened during any kind of disaster, big or small, life went on.

"You're lucky you live up so high," Helen told a robin that swooped down to perch on the branch of the rose of Sharon in the McCaffreys' front yard. "You don't have to worry about getting your feet wet."

When she reached the business district within a few blocks, she noted the sandbaggers at work again. They continued to shore up the storefronts, though the water barely splashed over the curbs. Sandwich-board signs had been propped up on the street, sandbags wrapped around the legs to keep them in place. *Slow Down,* they cautioned. *Haste Makes Wake.*

Helen couldn't help but crack a smile, thinking those looked a lot like the signs that usually resided at the docks, urging boaters to go slowly out of the harbor and into the river.

But her smile faded as she realized the signs wouldn't be needed at the harbor for a while, not until the flood-waters receded, which could take weeks. Then there would be such a mess to clean up afterward.

She sighed. It made her tired just to think of it.

"'Morning, Helen," Agnes said, popping out of her antiques shop. "Good thing you have your boots on. They're fitting, too. They make me want to *ribbit*."

Helen glanced down at the vibrant green galoshes with frog faces on the feet. Her granddaughter had sent them for her March birthday. "I think the water critters are the only ones enjoying things lately," she said.

Agnes nodded and set hands on hips. Helen noticed that her friend wasn't wearing a dress. She actually had on blue jeans, albeit dark ones that looked pressed. Helen couldn't remember the last time she'd seen anyone in jeans with creases. Instead of pumps, Agnes wore navy-blue Keds. She did spot pearls in the cleft of Agnes's collarbone between the lapels of her crisp linen blouse. There were pearl bobs clasped to her earlobes, as well. Even dressed down, Agnes knew how to look natty.

"How's business?" she asked.

"*What* business?" Agnes shrugged. "I'm getting everything upstairs that I can carry. By tomorrow I'll have my Closed sign up. It's not worth it. The TV weathermen are calling for the river to crest in the next week or two. The tourists are scared away. I'll just have to wheel and deal online for a while, until the river decides to play nice with us again."

The parking spots on either side of the street did look mostly empty. Two extended-cab pickup trucks with oversize tires had parked in front of the diner. Other than the sandbag crews, all the traffic seemed to be on foot, as the sidewalks had puddles but weren't underwater like the street.

"I'm thinking of moving to the top of the bluff," Helen said, only half joking.

"If I have to haul my inventory upstairs one more year, I'll go with you," Agnes replied. She started to turn toward the door to her shop but paused to ask, "Have you heard anything more about Luann Dupree? Is she coming back soon? You always seem to have your ear to the ground, so I thought maybe . . ."

"Nothing," Helen said. "Sorry."

"Hmm, that's odd, very odd. She never mentioned that she'd be going away," Agnes murmured. For a moment Helen thought she was going to add something more, but instead she waved a hand dismissively. "Well, I'm sure she'll be in touch when she's ready."

"Right."

"I'd best get back to work." Agnes nodded at Helen before she headed inside, the bells on the front door jangling as it dropped shut behind her.

Helen started toward the sheriff's office next door

to pick up the keys to the Historical Society. As she'd mentioned to Agnes, Luann Dupree had still not come back. Some were starting to gossip that she had gotten married in Las Vegas, and word had it that the town council was grumbling about replacing her. Art Beaner's wife, Bertha, had suggested to Helen that they were going to officially put Luann on unpaid administrative leave, or even fire her outright, unless she returned to River Bend within the week.

"Art's left her tons of voice mails, but she hasn't called back," Bertha had told Helen when they'd run into each other yesterday at the Cut 'n' Curl. "He did eventually get a text message saying she was deep in the Grand Canyon or some such place without good reception, so she'd be in touch in a few days."

If Luann truly loved her job as much as Sarah Biddle claimed she did, Helen was sure she'd come back rather than risk losing it. But if she *had* tied the knot in Vegas, maybe she didn't care. So far as Helen was aware, Luann had never been married before. Perhaps she'd decided it was time to focus on her personal life and put her career aside for a spell.

Stranger things had happened.

In the meantime, Helen had promised Clara that she'd continue their efforts to identify the subjects in the mountains of photographs, something Clara seemed truly passionate about. "It's one of the only things that I do to keep my mind off Betty and Bernie," her friend had confessed.

Helen had also promised Clara that she'd open up the Historical Society that morning since Clara had enough on her plate. Only when she let herself into Biddle's office, there was no sign of the sheriff or anyone else. No doubt he was out with the sandbagging crews. He'd probably be gone a good chunk of the day.

So she went over to his desk and tugged open the top drawer—where she'd seen Sarah Biddle drop the keys two days before—only to find a host of paper clips, rubber bands, pens with missing caps, and not much else. The Historical Society key ring was not there.

Helen could only surmise that Clara had beaten her to it. Perhaps she'd gotten up early and had wanted to get a head start. She did seem very dedicated to the project.

That thought in mind, Helen left the sheriff's office and made a beeline for the Historical Society building. Sure enough, the door was unlocked.

She went in and called out, "Clara, are you here?"

When no one answered, she hurried up the stairs and ducked her head into the makeshift storage room where they sorted the photographs. Though light streamed through the windows, the ceiling light wasn't on.

She flipped the switch.

"Clara?" she said again.

Then she heard the footsteps overhead in the renovated attic space where Luann Dupree lived—or *had* lived, depending on which gossip was doing the talking.

Helen had a good idea who it was, too.

She gripped the banister and ascended to the third floor, found the door wide-open, and marched inside.

"Oh, dear," she whispered.

Open boxes sat on the floor of Luann's small apartment as the sheriff's wife tossed things in willy-nilly. The place looked a disaster, like either a tornado had hit or someone was in the throes of moving.

"Sarah Biddle!" Helen said firmly, and the woman jumped, spinning about with one hand at her heart. "What in heaven's name are you doing with Luann's things?"

"Oh, Helen!" she cried out, eyes wide with shock. "Everything is such a mess! The mayor got an e-mail last night from Luann offering her resignation. He had Art Beaner call me at the crack of dawn to tell me to clear out the apartment since I'm Lu's best friend and she doesn't have family in the area. I'm supposed to put the boxes in storage until Luann shows up to claim them." Sarah rubbed a sleeve across her cheeks and sniffled. "This all feels so wrong."

The sheriff's wife wrung her hands as she stood in the middle of Luann's upended living-slash-dining room. Helen could feel her angst, and it settled like a knot inside her stomach. She picked her way through the mess and took Sarah's hand. Within a few steps, she'd led her to the small kitchen table and sat her down. Then she pulled up the other chair catty-corner.

"Take a deep breath," she advised. "Try to calm down."

Sarah did as much, but her eyes still filled with tears, and her cheeks remained flushed. "I'm okay, really."

Helen wasn't sure about that. But she asked anyway, "Have you heard from Luann directly?"

"I'm not sure how to answer that. All I've gotten are a few text messages that are pretty generic. Like, she's fine and dandy, and she's having fun with Mr. Maybe and to stop worrying, that kind of stuff."

"You haven't spoken to her, then?"

"No," Sarah said, sticking out her chin. "That's why I'm having a hard time believing this is on the up-and-up. I need to hear her voice. I want her to tell me that she's really in love and that she's finished with River Bend. I need to see a photo of her with this guy, making googly eyes at each other." She shook her head. "It's all wrong, Helen. The Luann I know wouldn't do anything this drastic without talking to me first. Something's happened to her. I can feel it in my bones. Why won't anyone listen?"

"I'm listening," Helen told her. She was a mother and a grandma. Listening was what she did.

"Here's what I don't get." Sarah rose from the chair and started to walk about the space. She pointed at the refrigerator first. "She'd gone grocery shopping last weekend. The fridge and freezer are full."

"She hadn't been on her date yet, though, had she?" Helen countered. "Sometimes all it takes is one moment to change everything. Expiration dates aren't going to matter."

Sarah pointed to a desk topped with papers and files. "Her laptop is gone, but she has a stack of bills that haven't been paid."

"Perhaps she'll pay them online. Isn't that what most people do these days?" Helen replied, although, personally, she didn't trust Internet banking or bill paying. She liked leaving a paper trail, even if she was the only one alive who still wrote checks and put stamps on envelopes.

"Okay, I'll give you that. But there's more that doesn't sit right with me."

"Lead on."

With a sniff, Sarah left the tiny living-and-dining area, walking beneath an open arch into the bedroom. Helen followed.

"She kept a suitcase under her bed, and it's gone, of course. But she hardly took anything with her," Sarah said, indicating neat piles of clothing settled on the duvet, shoes on the floor below. "I emptied her closet and drawers. Look at all the underwear, pajamas, slacks, blouses, pumps, you name it. It doesn't seem like she packed for more than a few days, and haphazardly at that."

"Clearly she didn't mean to be gone for long."

"Or maybe she didn't do her own packing." Sarah went over to the bureau, which appeared to have more atop it than was contained within the half-opened drawers. "She left good jewelry . . . pearls from her college graduation and rings her grandparents gave her that were important to her. When I took out the jewelry tray, I found her Social Security card and her birth certificate hidden beneath it."

"And she left her passport, as well," Helen added, having seen it in Sarah's hand the very day they'd learned Luann had flown the coop. "But are there any signs she didn't go willingly, any evidence of a struggle?"

"No," Sarah grudgingly admitted. "But what if she didn't have a chance to struggle? What if he caught her by surprise? He would have had to be crafty about it, because Luann was pretty tough. She flipped Frank flat on his back when he told her she wasn't cut out to be a volunteer deputy."

Helen had heard that story before. In fact, the whole town had heard it, and it had taken months for Frank Biddle to live it down. "My guess is that Luann went willingly."

"Maybe she did, at first. Maybe she thought she was just running off for the weekend, then *bam!* He slipped her a Mickey and she ended up stuck in a cellar," Sarah said, voice rattling. "Lu wouldn't give up her home and her job. She loved this place. Even if she was a closet romantic, she was not a complete flake."

"You *are* convinced, aren't you?" Helen said, because it was clear that Sarah wasn't going to be dissuaded from her theory that Luann had been abducted.

"I don't know what to do to convince Frank that he needs to investigate," Sarah replied. "He still says he can't help until I find some kind of proof that she's being held against her will. What does he expect me to show him? A ransom note made of cutout letters from magazines?"

"I know it must be hard, feeling like you're on the outside," Helen said, not sure how to console her. She'd been in Sarah's shoes before and understood what a stickler the sheriff could be when it came to doing things by the book.

Sarah sighed and turned away, waving hands around the room. "The mayor wants me to pack up Luann's belongings and move them out so they can hire a new director ASAP, but what am I supposed to do with everything? Frank will freak if I try to store this stuff in our garage forever. I guess I'll eventually have to get one of those pod things or a storage unit in Jerseyville."

"Didn't Luann provide any kind of forwarding address in her resignation e-mail?"

Sarah shook her head. "I didn't see the letter myself, but Art Beaner said it implied she was planning to travel indefinitely. He said she directed them to e-mail or text any messages, and to deposit her final paycheck electronically."

"You're right," Helen said. "It seems a bit odd that she doesn't want to communicate in a more personal way. Unless she's embarrassed by her actions and she's trying to avoid everyone."

"I've known Lu since the first grade," Sarah said, voice cracking. "When her folks divorced during junior high and she clammed up, I was the only one who could get her to talk. I was the first one she called when her senior prom date dumped her and ran off with the cheerleader he'd knocked up."

Helen made a vague "mm-hmm" noise.

"Yes, she kept a lot to herself," Sarah added. "So she's a bit of a loner. She'd rather hang out with dusty old relics than people, and she's definitely not one for ladies' lunches or gossip sessions. But I'm the best friend she's got. Why would she be afraid to face me over something like this?"

"I've got a suggestion," she said.

The sheriff's wife perked up. "What is it?"

"Could you text her with a message that might trip up someone who doesn't know her that well? Like asking how her arthritis is . . ."

"But she doesn't have arthritis."

"Right," Helen said, nodding.

Sarah wrinkled her brow. "I took a similar tack already, asking if she remembered that her uncle Bob was due to pass through town this week, which he isn't, of course, because she doesn't have an Uncle Bob."

"What kind of response did you get?"

"The text said that nothing could make her come back yet."

"So either it's really Luann or it's a very clever captor."

"Seems that way," Sarah agreed. "Then I asked her to send photos from her travels, but she claimed the camera on her phone isn't working. So I mentioned that her boyfriend could post pictures from his phone to Facebook, and I got a message saying he'd dropped off social media so he could focus on her, and she had gotten off, too."

"Oh, dear," Helen said.

"How am I ever going to know if it's Luann and not . . ." Sarah hesitated.

*Her lover? Her kidnapper?*

Helen wasn't sure how to fill in the blank.

"I don't know," she replied.

"Exactly." Sarah sighed. "I can't help wondering if she's in a pickle she can't get out of, and I think I'm the only one in town who cares."

Helen couldn't fault the skeptics, since she herself was among them. It would have been impossible *not* to be skeptical with so many unanswered questions, namely, why would anyone forcibly take Luann Dupree? She was the director of a small-town historical society, not a blue blood. If someone had snatched her looking for ransom, why send texts to her best friend reassuring her that all was fine? Why wasn't the kidnapper demanding money?

Helen voiced her thoughts aloud. "Why would someone abduct Luann and pretend she's run away? Why keep up the charade?"

"I've been wondering that myself," Sarah said, "and there's only one thing I can figure out."

"What?"

"He wants whatever it is she stumbled upon when she starting unpacking all those old boxes after the renovation. I think she must have told him about it, and maybe he knew what it was worth and decided to shake her down."

"But you don't know what it is?"

"Not yet," Sarah said, and her gaze darted about. "I haven't found anything up here that looks valuable, but it may very well be in this building, right?"

"Still, how will you know when you find it?"

Sarah shrugged. "I'm not sure. But he must have known about it. Could be she was asking questions about it on some historical-nerds site and he latched on to her. That's how lots of these creeps work. They target women, pretend to want a relationship, and then they bleed them dry. Frank was just telling me the other day that romance scams make up the highest percentage of online fraud."

"So you're convinced her Internet beau is a fake and he just wanted something she had," Helen said, putting it simply. "What happens to her if he found it?"

"Then Luann's probably toast, and her body's going to turn up in the dumpster at a random truck stop along the highway."

"Sarah!" Helen chided. "Let's think more positively, shall we? If this mystery man wanted to pilfer a long-lost antiquity, you'd think he would have ransacked the place before he took Luann, right?" she said, recalling that the sheriff had taken stock of the place the morning after Luann disappeared, and nothing had seemed awry except for the puddle that had seeped beneath a back door.

"But why bother ransacking the place if he had Lu?" Sarah countered. "Wouldn't it be easier to find the artifact if he kidnapped her and got her to cough up the location? We know he's got her phone, and he must have taken her laptop, too. All her notes are probably on there."

Helen couldn't argue with that.

"If he's got her keys, he can pop back in and retrieve it in the middle of the night, and no one would even realize it was gone." She suddenly stopped talking, and her expression turned stricken. "It's my fault, isn't it? I told her not to go alone on that date. I should have followed them, shouldn't I? It's like a horror flick after all."

"It's not your fault."

"This is terrible." Sarah groaned and went back to biting her lip.

It was terrible, all right.

Helen wasn't sure if the sheriff's wife was truly onto something, or if she was so upset about her best girl-friend's abrupt departure that she'd gone and lost her mind.

## Chapter 8

HELEN WAS ALMOST relieved when Sarah Biddle took off in search of more packing boxes. At least the sheriff's wife wasn't just spouting off wild theories about Luann anymore. Instead she was a woman on a mission. She swore she'd track down the mysterious artifact, which she was sure would provide clues to whatever had happened to Luann.

For Sarah's sake, Helen hoped that Luann would call soon or send a smiling selfie from the Grand Canyon or Yosemite, wherever she'd wandered off to with her paramour, anything to reassure her frantic BFF that everything was fine.

But she had to admit Sarah's doubts didn't seem entirely unfounded, and she couldn't fault her for wanting to play detective. She'd done it herself a time or two, mostly with the intention of helping loved ones out of trouble. But this time, she decided to leave the meddling to Sarah. After all, the woman was married to the sheriff, who should rightly get involved if Sarah's instincts proved on target. Helen had enough to worry about with the flood and Clara's family troubles.

And besides, she had another task at hand, and she decided to get to it, even though Clara hadn't shown up yet. With Sarah gone and silence her only company, she went down to the second floor and settled herself at the table where she and Clara had been working in the days prior. She reached for the nearest pile of photos, finding a pack that was rubber-banded together.

She unbound them and shuffled through a few, trying to pin down the subject matter. Soon she came upon a series of black-and-white shots depicting balloons released to the sky. Postcards dangled from the strings. Faces tipped heavenward, as though to watch their progress.

"It's Children's Day," she said aloud, recognizing the Balloon Ascension specifically.

River Bend still celebrated similarly to this day, and Helen herself had filled out numerous cards through the years for her own kids as well as for herself. When the balloons were let go, they traveled near and far. When someone in a distant town found the self-addressed postcard caught on their fence or snagged on a stalk of corn in their field, they returned it. The mayor kept track of all the postmarks on a map to ascertain where the farthest balloon had landed. The winner received an assortment of items from local businesses, anything from suitcases to haircuts or meals at the diner.

Helen continued skimming through a half-dozen similar photos, finding a few marked on the back with an August date from sixty-odd years prior.

Since it was more than a decade before she and Joe had moved to town, the pictures belonged in Clara's pile. She started to push the photos over to the opposite side of the table but stopped.

A face caught her eye—two faces, actually—and she drew the stack back in front of her. There were two girls in the photograph, one in her teens and the other in her twenties, standing on a porch festooned with bunting. They seemed poised to watch the Children's Day parade.

She adjusted her glasses on the edge of her nose and smiled.

*Could it be . . . ?*

Helen chuckled. Yes, it was, just as she'd thought.

Clara couldn't have been more than sixteen, Helen surmised. The girl frowned at the camera, her brow creased beneath her dark bobbed and pinned hair. An oversized plaid shirt hung down over her pedal push-ers, as if to hide her ample body. Beside her stood her blond sister, Betty, older by a decade, tall and thin in short sleeves and rolled-up jeans belted snugly at the waist. She was a sharp contrast to Clara's petite height and stocky build. A twentysomething Bernie stood in Betty's shadow, smiling shyly, his dark hair pomaded and brushed off his brow.

On the other side of the porch, a gruff-looking man leaned a hand on the railing. He had his other arm slung around a middle-aged woman, whose frown seemed to mirror Clara's. Helen had never known Clara's parents but assumed that was them.

Hmm.

It wasn't the happiest family portrait Helen had ever seen. But she was sure Clara would get a kick out of finding it there with all the photographs from that long-ago Children's Day. Helen hoped she herself would stumble upon some candid family shots of her own brood when they were younger.

"What are you staring at so intently?"

Hearing her friend's voice over her shoulder gave Helen a start.

"Clara!" She laughed. "You won't believe whose photo I just found. There's a girl I know who's far too young to look so unhappy. Or maybe that's just what teenagers have always done."

"What teenaged girl?" Clara dropped her tote bag to the floor and settled into the chair.

Helen picked up the photo and pushed it across the table.

Her friend made sure her glasses were on her nose before she took the picture and gave it a thorough once-over.

Instead of seeing delight on her face, Helen saw something else. It wasn't horror exactly, but it was close. A flicker of fear or maybe anger that lit up Clara's blue eyes; the settling of her lips into a hard line; and the intake of breath that seemed held for an eternity before Clara released it.

"It's your family, isn't it?" Helen said, feeling as if she'd done something wrong. So she started to babble when her friend remained silent. "That's you and Betty, yes? And Bernie's standing there behind her. I never knew your parents, but I can see you in your mother's face. As for your father . . ."

"That's not my father." Clara's chin snapped up. "He was my stepfather."

"I didn't know."

"My father died when I was six and Betty was sixteen. My mother remarried a year after. She didn't know how to manage on her own and pretty much fell apart." Clara's full cheeks flushed. "Betty kind of took over with me after that."

Helen watched her friend as she spoke. Clara's face went through a mess of contortions, as though she was fighting hard to remain stoic and losing the battle.

"When he moved into the house, it was . . . difficult," Clara explained quietly. "Betty couldn't stand him. She married Bernie as soon as she was out of high school. She moved away, and I was devastated. It was a hard time those years without her, a really hard time."

There was little Helen could do but reach over and give Clara's hand a squeeze. But Clara slipped her fingers away to touch the photograph.

"I went to live with Betty and Bernie in Coal City

when I was sixteen, not long after that summer. Bernie was gone a lot, traveling for the coal company. Betty took me in when I didn't know where else to turn. She kept me from screwing up my life. I'd do anything for her, Helen." Her glasses fogged up, and Clara removed them, wiping them on her floral-print dress. "I owe her so much."

"I'm sorry for what you went through, hon. I really am," Helen said.

How could she have known Clara for so long and never heard this sad tale? But it was a private matter, the sort of thing you didn't ask about. One of those locked-up secrets that stayed tucked away until something shook it loose.

Clara made a noise, like a strangled breath. "It was so long ago. I try hard not to dwell on it. It's easier that way."

"It's wonderful that you had Betty when you needed her most," she remarked. "And that Betty has you now."

"You're right about that," Clara said, looking uncomfortable, like she was ready to change the subject. "Hey, have you heard any news about Luann Dupree? Is she really not coming back?"

And change the subject she did.

Helen thought about sharing her run-in with Sarah Biddle not twenty minutes before. She could easily repeat what she'd learned about Luann, but she reined herself in. She wasn't in the mood to gossip. She was thinking of a sixteen-year-old girl living in a house with a difficult man who wasn't her father and a mother who'd fallen apart, and her heart ached too much to talk nonsense.

When Helen hesitated, Clara remarked, "You do know something."

"All I know for sure is that she's still gone."

"Oh. That's bad news for the Historical Society, but I guess it's good if she's happy." Clara shrugged. "I wonder if they'll replace her."

"I imagine they will, if she's not coming back."

"It's so odd, isn't it?" Clara murmured and shook her gray pin curls.

"Yes, it's odd, indeed," Helen agreed.

"Well, I figure whoever's in charge is still going to want to archive all these photos, right? So how about we schlep through a hundred more in the next hour or two then hit the diner for lunch? I'm craving the cheesy tomato soup and a piece of apple pie."

Helen smiled. "I'm in."

She turned to reach for another pile of photographs from the white carton near her chair, and from the corner of her eye saw Clara slipping the photograph of her family into her tote bag beneath the table.

*That isn't yours,* she nearly said. *It belongs to the Historical Society.*

But Helen stopped herself. If Clara wanted to keep a painful moment in her past from being part of the archives, she understood.

So she said nothing.

*After the Flood*

## Chapter 9

*Monday, Three Weeks Later*

TWEEEET.

Helen's phone trilled from her bedside table, awakening her on the first ring. The second twitter roused—and frightened—a slumbering Amber. He flipped from his back to his paws in no time flat. An involuntary "oomph" escaped Helen's lips as the twenty-pound tom used her belly as a springboard before diving off the bed.

*Tweeeet.*

She caught the phone before the third ring, scooping up the receiver from its charging cradle and hitting the Talk button.

"Um-hmm?" she mumbled, still not fully alert.

"Oh, Helen!" It was Clara, and she was beside herself. "Something dreadful has happened! I'm taking Betty to see the sheriff right now! Can you meet us there?"

"What's going on?" Helen sat up in bed, blinking

the sleep from her eyes and trying to clear the cobwebs from her head. She glanced at the alarm clock. It was eight fifteen. She'd slept later than usual after staying up half the night racing to the finish of a mystery. "You said the sheriff's office? Are you in trouble?"

"No, it's not me! It's Bernie."

"Bernie's been arrested?"

"No, it's worse than that! Please, hurry!" Clara got out in a strangled tone before hanging up.

Helen stared at the phone in her hand for a minute before finally setting the handset back on the charging cradle.

Something had happened to Bernie.

*Bernie Winston,* Helen reminded her soggy brain, Betty Winston's husband. He was Clara's brother-in-law who used to work in the coal industry, the one with Alzheimer's who'd been a mainstay in River Bend gossip these past weeks. If talk wasn't about the flood or Luann Dupree running off with her lover, folks were gabbing about glimpsing Bernie standing in the window of his house in his underpants or slipping out and turning up in a neighbor's backyard, sitting on a patio chair.

Helen found herself wondering if Bernie had managed to find the car keys that Betty had reportedly hidden away and had driven into someone or something. That had always been one of Clara's worst fears.

*Oh, dear.*

Her adrenaline kicked in.

She threw off the covers and raced to her bureau

then pulled open drawers to retrieve socks, bra, and T-shirt. She shrugged out of her nightgown, dressed quickly, and grabbed yesterday's warm-up suit from the bench at the end of her bed. She raced to the bathroom to brush teeth and splash water on her face.

All the while Amber sat in the hallway, silently watching and waiting, his tail doing an anxious tic.

"I'll open a can when I get back!" she assured him, knowing he'd hardly starve in her absence since she always left a bowl of dry food on the kitchen floor.

She had to leave by the back door, as the creek had spilled over onto Jersey Avenue the week before. Though the water wasn't more than ankle-high, Helen had to don her rubber boots every time she left the house. Still, she cut through the side yard and marched upward until she reached Granite Avenue. The asphalt and gravel on that street was still dry.

Helen hurried along the sidewalk, her head down, not glancing at the Victorian cottages on either side of her, simply focused on moving her legs forward and getting to Main Street as fast as she could.

By the time she reached the heart of River Bend—a mere two blocks that composed the tiny downtown—she was breathing hard. Beneath the morning sun, she could see the slick sheen of water that covered the road's surface. It rippled every time a car drove slowly through it.

Helen looked both ways before crossing the road, wincing at the feel of river mud beneath her boots.

When she flung open the door to Frank Biddle's

office, she spied the sheriff at his desk, hands pumping the air in front of him as if trying to stop traffic.

Standing before him were Clara Foley and her older sister, Betty Winston. Both seemed to be talking at the same time, arms flailing.

They clearly hadn't heard Helen enter, though she'd come just in time to catch Clara howling, "You must get help and be quick before something bad happens," while Betty pleaded, "Please, Sheriff, he doesn't know left from right these days. You have to find him before he gets hurt!"

*Be quick before something happens? Find him before he gets hurt?*

"What's going on?" she asked, though she had a feeling she knew what it was, and it wasn't the car accident she'd imagined.

The sheriff rose from his chair, tenting his fingers on his desk. "Morning, Mrs. Evans," he said, seeming grateful for the interruption.

Clara and Betty stopped talking at once and turned as Helen approached.

"Oh, Helen," Clara moaned and hustled toward her, catching her elbow and drawing her near. Clara's blue eyes were red rimmed and tired. Her broad face frowned, dimpled chin trembling. "Bernie's wandered off again, and this time we can't find him," she blurted out, and Betty let out a whimper. "We're afraid he's gotten himself lost in the woods, and with the river rising so fast, who knows what could happen! If he can't recall how to tie his shoes, how could he remember how to swim if he fell into the harbor or a swollen creek?"

At which point Betty's mewls became a gut-wrenching sob, and she turned the palest shade of white Helen had ever seen.

"Mrs. Winston, are you all right?" the sheriff said, taking a step nearer. "Should I call Doc Melville?"

"I could fetch him myself," Helen volunteered because the Melvilles' place was only a few blocks away.

"No," Betty said weakly, waving them off with a wobbly hand. "I'm perfectly fi—" she got out before her eyelids fluttered like window shades flapping. Then her eyes rolled up into her head, and she began to crumple.

Despite his paunch, Frank Biddle had reflexes like a cat. Helen heard the sheriff grunt as he rounded his desk and lunged forward, catching the frail-looking woman around her waist just before she fainted dead away.

## Chapter 10

BETTY WINSTON PERCHED upon a lumpy sofa in the sheriff's office. She held a cup of water in her trembling hands and tried hard to bring it to her lips. As she sipped, a few drops splattered onto her lime-green pedal pushers. Though she was eighty years old, she felt like a toddler learning to drink from a grown-up glass as water sloshed down her chin.

Embarrassed, she wiped the dribble away with the back of her hand.

*Calm down, old girl,* she told herself. She wasn't doing anybody any good by behaving like a wilting violet.

"Here, let me have that."

Helen Evans came out of her chair and took the cup away before Betty spilled the whole thing in her lap.

"Thank you," she whispered because water wasn't what she needed to soothe her. She needed Bernie back, safe and sound, locked snugly inside the house, where she could keep an eye on him.

*This shouldn't be happening.*

None of this should have happened. It wasn't fair.

"Take a deep breath, Betts," Clara said quietly. Her younger sister sat beside her and reached over with a plump hand, gently patting her thigh. "Then tell Sheriff Biddle exactly what you told me."

Betty did just that: she drew in a belly-bloating breath and expelled it. Still, she couldn't get anything past her throat but a sad little sob.

So the sheriff waded in. He pulled a chair up and leaned forward, his forearms braced on his thighs as he spoke. "You said Bernie's missing. He didn't take a car, by chance?"

Betty shook her head. That one was easy enough. She somehow found her voice to reply, "No, thank God. He doesn't drive anymore. I hid his keys last year before he killed somebody. I'd like to sell the darned car, but I don't know who'd buy it."

"You should see it," Clara chimed in. "Betty might end up having to donate it for scrap. Bernie dinged both bumpers and knocked the side mirrors off. Makes you wonder, doesn't it, what he kept hitting when he was still cruising around. The DMV didn't care that he had Alzheimer's," she insisted. "They let him drive so long as his license hadn't expired. Betty finally had to take a stand all by herself, and Bernie was not too pleased. He threw tantrums for weeks until he forgot he had a car."

Sheriff Biddle listened without flinching. "I sympathize with what you've gone through. It's a no-win situation," he agreed and turned his focus back to Betty. "So he wandered off on foot?"

Betty nodded. "Yes, he must have. There's no other way for him to get around. I try to watch him, but I can't keep an eye on him every moment."

"Of course you can't," Clara told her. "You'd have to have eyes in the back of your head for that."

"But he's never wandered so far before that I couldn't find him," she said pointedly, and her gaze shifted from the sheriff to Helen Evans. "He mostly sticks close to home except that once when he walked up to Grafton."

"Oh, but they all disappear sooner or later, don't they?" Clara said and patted her hand. "It's part of the disease, and hardly the worst of it. Well, that's what the article that I read online said, anyway."

Sometimes Betty wanted to tell Clara to hush up. Saying exactly what she thought—no matter how honest—didn't always make things better.

"When exactly did you realize he was gone, ma'am?" the sheriff asked.

"It wasn't soon enough," Betty said and cringed, feeling the need to explain so the sheriff didn't peg her as a bad wife. "We were up early, around six o'clock, so I left him in front of the TV while I started the laundry," she began, and Frank Biddle nodded, encouraging. "We weren't planning on going anywhere today. I needed to catch up on the housework, which is why I told Ellen we couldn't go to the Science Center even though Sawyer has a day off. Besides, it's hard for Bernie to be on his feet for too long with his new hips. That's another reason I never imagined he'd take off like he did."

"Ellen is your daughter, isn't she, ma'am?" the sheriff asked, and Betty realized she'd been babbling.

"Yes, she and her husband live in St. Louis with my granddaughter, Sawyer. I called Ellen when I couldn't find Bernie." Betty heard her own voice rattle. "They're on their way in from the city now."

The sheriff cleared his throat. "You said you were doing laundry while Bernie watched television . . ."

"Oh, yes, I'm sorry," Betty said, wrinkling her brow. She had lost track and tried to recall where she'd left off. "I'd turned on the rerun of last night's Cardinals game, because Bernie couldn't remember who'd won even though we'd watched it the first time. He had his eyes on the TV, like he was taking it in, although I could turn on bowling or golf and it wouldn't matter. He can even stare at the screen for hours when the TV's off." She paused to gnaw her lower lip. "I was up and down to the basement laundry room, and I did some mopping in the kitchen. I heard the noise of the television the whole time. So I don't know when he slipped out." She felt her eyes well. "Best I can guess he's been gone an hour or more. I tried looking for him myself . . ."

"And when she couldn't track him down, she called me, and I went right over," Clara butted in, lacing her steady fingers with Betty's trembling ones. "I double-checked every room in the house. Then while Betty phoned the neighbors, I walked up and down the street, calling out and knocking on doors. Finally, we got in my car and drove through the whole town and up the River Road to Grafton and back, but we didn't see him. That's why we came here."

"I've got signs all over the house telling Bernie not to open doors or answer phones, but it's all futile at this point," Betty pointed out, picking up where her sister left off. "He can't really read much, and he couldn't remember our address to save his life. I made a card for his wallet with vital information, but he only carries a few dollars' cash and no credit cards. I had to do that after he got us into a few financial pickles."

She stopped talking, feeling embarrassed.

"Those things happen," Helen said, giving her a sympathetic glance. "It's common for folks to try to take advantage when they realize someone's mind isn't really all there."

"Yes," Betty agreed. "It is."

"I apologize if this sounds rude, ma'am," Frank Biddle said and doffed his cap to scratch at the sparse hair across his scalp. "But your husband's Alzheimer's is pretty advanced at this point, is that right?"

"Yes."

"How far along is it?"

"He was diagnosed six years ago," Betty told him, and she felt relieved to say it. "At first it was just misplacing things and forgetting names. But he's been slipping pretty fast this past year. He says the strangest things. Sometimes it's hurtful even though I'm sure he doesn't mean it." She hesitated, looking at Clara. "It's like his real memories get confused with fiction."

Clara met her eyes, and Betty knew she understood exactly what she meant. Her sister cleared her throat, her grip tightening on Betty's hand. "I would say Bernie's in Stage Six."

"And how many stages are there, if you don't mind my asking?" the sheriff asked, cocking his head.

"Seven," Clara said solemnly.

"I see." Frank Biddle nodded.

Betty heard pity in those two small words, and it hit her hard in the chest. She closed her eyes as tears stung them, hanging on to her sister's hand and feeling the same sense of helplessness that had stricken her since Bernie's diagnosis. Betty had thought surviving all those miscarriages in the early years of their marriage and the breast cancer a decade ago was hard enough, that nothing else could possibly get to them.

Then Bernie had his hips replaced, and he'd started acting oddly. Initially she'd figured he was going deaf, as often as he repeated questions or parts of conversation. But his ears had tested fine. Her husband had always been sharp as a tack—he had a master's degree in civil engineering—so she'd laid the blame on other things: not enough sleep, too much wine, the anesthesia from his hip surgeries.

She had not wanted to believe it was dementia,

not until the day the Grafton police had called Sheriff Biddle when Bernie had taken a stroll up the River Road and couldn't remember how to get back.

She had known then what it had meant, even before they'd seen the neurologist and he'd confirmed it. Nothing had been the same since that day. Bernie was still alive, still with her—unlike the husbands of many of River Bend's resident widows, Helen and Clara among them—but Betty had lost him just the same.

"Are you all right, Mrs. Winston?" Frank Biddle asked. "Are you sure I can't fetch Doc Melville?"

"I don't need the doctor," Betty said and forced her chin up to meet the sheriff's gaze. She didn't care how her voice shook. "But the answer is no, I'm not all right. I've been with Bernie for more than sixty of my eighty years, and there are days he doesn't even know who I am. Sometimes his eyes stare right through me." She wiped tears from her cheeks. "His mind can retrieve bits and pieces from the past that he thinks are his present. He'll tell me he wrenched his knee playing football, which he hasn't done since high school, or he'll say that he's wearing his lucky socks to accept an award for science, which he won in junior high. He tells strangers to call him Win, which his best friend in school used to call him. But I'd never even heard that nickname before. It's like he's a different person."

Tears surged anew into her eyes, and she blinked hard to fight them off.

"Alzheimer's is a terrible thing to go through," Helen

remarked from her chair catty-corner. She sat so attentively: her back ramrod straight, her gray head cocked, and pale eyes narrowed. "Sometimes I think it's harder on the caregiver than the patient."

"It's devastated the whole family," Clara added so forcefully that the loose skin beneath her chin quivered.

Betty sniffed, trying to hold herself together. "The other night he said deer were running down the hallway, when there was nothing there at all. Sometimes before I go to bed, he asks if I have a ride home." She paused, pinching at the bridge of her nose. "He thinks we're at a cocktail party, that he lives with his mother, not me. I feel like I'm losing my mind right along with him."

A sob hitched itself in Betty's throat, and she stopped talking. She shook her head, biting down on a trembling lip.

"It's okay," Clara whispered. "You don't always have to be strong, you know."

"Oh, I'm not," Betty said, and a sad little laugh escaped. "I'm definitely not."

Clara squeezed her fingers so hard Betty winced and then her sister's hold loosened the littlest bit. "I'm always here for you, Betts, whatever you need."

"I know." Betty glanced down, appreciating the sturdiness of her sister's grip, the way her own thin hand looked so small within Clara's plump one. How many times through the years had they been there for each other like this? she wondered, knowing it was too many to count. Her life would have been very different without her sister giving up so much for her, she mused, though she was sure Clara would insist it was Betty who'd sacrificed most.

"You have done all you could," Clara said pointedly as Betty lifted her head. "Don't feel guilty for an instant. Most wives would have put their husbands in a nursing home by now. I'm not sure how you do it all without collapsing."

"Clara's right. It's not your fault," Helen said, her brow creased with sympathy. "The sheriff will use every means at his disposal to bring Bernie home safely."

"I aim to do just that, Mrs. Winston, but I'll need more information, if you don't mind," Frank Biddle remarked, tucking a finger in his collar and tugging. "Can you go home and get me a recent photograph of your husband?"

"Well, I have one right here, Sheriff." Betty wiggled her hand free of Clara's and fished inside her small handbag.

She'd always carried a picture of Bernie in her wallet. If she were more comfortable with technology, she'd likely have dozens on her phone. Ellen was always scrolling through the latest photos of Sawyer on hers. But it felt so impersonal to Betty. Didn't anyone ever make prints anymore and put them in frames or in a scrapbook? Betty couldn't quite grasp the notion of storing an album of photos on a cloud. So far as she was concerned, tech clouds were as nebulous as the white fluff in the sky. A change of weather—or a glitch in the system—and *poof*, they were gone.

"Will this do?" she asked and handed the picture to Biddle.

"Yep, that'll work," he said with one quick glance at the photograph. "Let me scan and enlarge it, and we'll be in business."

With a grunt, he got up, walked over to his desk, and fiddled with a piece of equipment that looked like a small copy machine. Tapping a few keys on his computer made the machine began to whir. Over its noise, he asked, "Can you tell me what Bernie was wearing when you last saw him?"

Betty didn't have to think very hard to answer that one. "He had on blue jeans, white sneakers, and a pale blue golf shirt."

He would have worn the same thing day after day if Betty didn't take his clothes from his closet and wash them. Bernie didn't know the difference between dirty and clean and hung everything up at the end of the day just the same. He'd even put damp pants away if he'd had an accident in them, which was becoming more frequent of late. Betty wrinkled her nose, thinking of the smell. Bernie had become a different man from the fastidious man she'd married, though she realized it wasn't his fault. It was his damned disease.

"He'll be home soon, Betts, you'll see," Clara said quietly.

But Betty didn't just want Bernie to come home.

She wanted the *old* Bernie back, she thought, and tears rolled down her cheeks.

"You okay to answer a few more questions, ma'am?" Biddle asked.

Betty brushed a sleeve against her face. "Yes, of course."

Still seated as his desk, the sheriff quizzed her about Bernie's height and weight, and Betty heard the *click-clack* of his fingers on the keyboard. Within a few minutes, he'd finished whatever he was doing, removed the photograph from the scanner, and brought it back to her.

"I've put out a Silver Alert on your husband. Everyone in the county with a cell phone will get a text message," he said as Betty slowly rose from the couch. "I'll get my volunteer deputies on the horn, and we'll search the town and the woods for Bernie," he assured her, and Betty hung onto Clara as they headed toward the door.

"He's like a child, Sheriff," Betty said. "He won't know how to get home on his own."

"We won't stop until we locate him, ma'am, I promise you that."

Betty pursed her lips and nodded as Clara walked her out. She wanted desperately to believe everything was going to be fine. But deep inside, she knew it wouldn't be, not ever again.

## Chapter 11

THE RIVER HAD risen several feet more in the past week alone, though John Danielson had no intention of postponing his trek into the stretch of woods beyond Springfield Avenue. He'd been planning it since the day he'd been hired by the River Bend town council to take over as director of the Historical Society. Once he'd read through Luann Dupree's notes about Lerner's cabin with accompanying photographs, he knew he had to see it for himself.

The simple log cabin took two weeks to build, and while he worked on it, Jacques Lerner lived in a wigwam procured from a friendly member of a local tribe. Lerner did most of the work on the cabin himself, though he did have help in order to make the cabin larger than he would have been able to do on his own. His assistance came from random transients with whom he conducted business, both settlers living in the Mississippi River Valley and the Native Americans who'd preceded them. When the cabin was finished, Lerner was said to have thrown a party that lasted a week, at least according to a newspaper article from 1805 that suggested explorer Meriwether Lewis attended the festivities (although since the guests were purportedly drinking home-brewed elderberry wine, among other Native concoctions, this sighting of Meriwether Lewis may well be an exaggeration).

Perusing the description of the cabin and its connection to Meriwether Lewis and William Clark had given John goose bumps. He felt the hair on his arms prickle even now.

He thought suddenly of a snippet from a journal entry by Clark before the expedition that had been printed out and tacked up on the board behind the Historical Society director's desk.

We all believe that we are about to enter on the most perilous and difficult part of our voyage, yet I see no one repining; all appear ready to meet those difficulties which await us with resolution and becoming fortitude.

John puffed out his chest, feeling some of that fortitude ebbing through him.

After cutting through the cul-de-sac where Springfield ended, he hiked toward the creek, walking parallel to the stream through the tangle of shrubs and trees. He would have followed the creek bed itself, which Luann's notes mentioned usually ran dry, except the stream had swollen over its banks, forcing John deeper into the thicket.

If truth be told, the flooded path merely added an element of danger that made his heart race. He felt like a long-ago explorer, looking for a lost city or pirate booty or the Fountain of Youth. Though his sights weren't set on any of the above but on the old log cabin built by French fur trader Jacques Lerner. According to the letters and diary entries that were part of the Historical Society archives, Lerner had purportedly left gold or other treasure buried thereabouts. The idea of finding that treasure made John's heart race, as well.

It was one of the reasons he'd been so eager to move to River Bend. The valley was teeming with tall tales and ghost stories about trappers and furriers and Indians and French explorers. For a history buff, that kind of juicy lore was akin to dangling a carrot in front of a hungry horse, and John couldn't resist.

"Whoa!"

A branch snagged his hat, and he pinched the brim, holding it down as he ducked beneath the grabby limb.

He trudged ahead through the muddy slop in knee-high rain boots, a bandanna tied around his neck and the brown wool fedora on his head.

A month ago he'd been lecturing on Ancient Greece and the Roman Empire to slouching adolescents who paid more attention to their text messages than their textbooks. It had maddened him wasting his breath when he knew he wasn't so much a molder of minds as a glorified babysitter.

But that was then, and this was now.

Finally, he felt as though Fortune was smiling down on him instead of just blowing him a raspberry.

He breathed in fresh air that smelled of spring—things green and ripe—with just a hint of damp earth and decay. He had to fight to keep from laughing aloud, although it wouldn't have mattered. Who would have heard him this deep in the woods?

Who would have ever thought that he'd find his dream in this Podunk river town? But, by God, he was living it.

From the time he was a kid, John had wanted to be Indiana Jones.

Ever since he'd watched Harrison Ford fleeing from poisoned-arrow-slinging Pygmies on-screen at the Lincoln Theatre in Belleville when he was ten, he'd wished like mad that he could run away from school and wing his way halfway around the world. What could be cooler, he wondered, than prowling through the jungle, hunting for missing treasure?

As a teenager, he'd fallen in love with King Tut and envisioned joining an archaeological dig in Egypt. He'd read every book in his school library about pharaohs and mummies and pyramids. He'd concocted his own set of hieroglyphics and carved made-up messages into the cinderblock walls in the basement until his stepfather had found them and told him to stop.

As he'd grown older and more grounded in reality, John had come to grips with the fact that he couldn't travel anywhere beyond a tank of gas and the shaky suspension on his rusty old Chevy pickup. So his fascination had shifted away from Northern Africa and the Middle East and toward more familiar turf: the Mississippi River Valley. When John was a senior in high school, his AP History instructor had taken a few select students to the Cahokia Mounds during some test excavations. John had been eager to help on the dig. He'd envisioned sifting through sediment and finding incredible Native American artifacts.

Only he quickly discovered that he didn't like assisting on the dig very much. It was slow, tedious work measured more in inches than feet. And it was hot work, too, unbearably so, particularly in the summertime. John couldn't imagine Indiana Jones standing in the sun week after week, painstakingly filtering dirt through a screen only to turn up a button some tourist had lost fifty years before.

So instead of becoming an archaeologist, John had settled for reading about exciting discoveries of ancient civilizations in *Archaeology Magazine* (his mother had gifted him a lifetime subscription for his college graduation). And he'd earned his teaching certificate so he could share his love of history with kids who dreamed of becoming Indiana Jones, too.

But after surviving twenty years of middle-school politics and students who were mostly indifferent to the ancient Egyptian dynasties—and John didn't have an app for that—he'd started looking for another gig, something less dispiriting that would stimulate his passion for history.

Taking over as director of a small-town historical society had seemed a fitting answer to his long-standing prayer. John had known precisely where River Bend sat: in a valley between the bluffs along the Mississippi, not twenty minutes north of Alton. He'd driven past it often enough as a child. His mother had frequently taken him to Pere Marquette Park, past the lighthouse of River Bend, where John had loved poking around for arrowheads left behind by the Illini Indians who had once lived in the very spot where the park's lodge was built.

When the spot in River Bend had opened up, John had pounced on the opportunity. He'd polished his curriculum vitae and scored an interview with the 91-year-old mayor and a few of the town council members. Oddly enough, they'd seemed less impressed with his résumé than the fact that he was clean shaven and wore pressed Dockers, button-down shirt, and tie.

"First tie I've seen today," Mayor Plunkett had sputtered between sips of what looked like prune juice. "Kids these days wear full beards like mountain men who can't find their razors, and they sure as shootin' don't know how to dress up. We had a feller in this morning who was wearing his pajama pants. They had a giant sponge-man on 'em. Looked ridiculous."

John stifled a grin, wondering if the elderly mayor considered him a "kid" when he was on the north side of forty.

"They all want to work from home, too, which usually means the basement of their parents' house," the mayor added and squinted at John with rheumy eyes. "You don't still live with your mother, do you?"

"No, sir, I don't," John said even though he'd doubted that question was actually legal.

"You don't mind moving to River Bend with your family?" the chairman of the board, a fellow named Art Beaner, piped up. "Our population skews more AARP than Toys"R"Us."

"I don't have a family," John had replied, "and I like being around folks older than myself. I'd rather hear about the past than the present."

"Just so you don't meet some sweetheart online and decide to run off like your predecessor," the mayor said with a harrumph, shaking his knobby head.

His predecessor being Luann Dupree, about whom John had heard plenty during the course of his interview. She had taken off abruptly, leaving things in disarray in the midst of several ongoing projects. And since the Historical Society's director was the sole paid human on staff, there was no one to pick up the slack.

Mr. Beaner gave the mayor a sideways glance before clarifying, "Not that we could restrict you from communicating with anyone online, of course. What you do on your own time is your business."

"I understand your concern, but I'm not about to run off anywhere," John had said, because he really didn't care to date, not seriously. If Indiana Jones had stayed away from women, he would have found himself in far fewer life-threatening situations. So unless John ran into the reincarnation of Cleopatra or Nefertiti, he didn't figure he'd find a female worth the expense of an engagement ring. "I like to save my focus for my work," he told his potential employers. "I pretty much live and breathe history."

"Sounds like a winner to me." The mayor had nodded and popped an unlit cigar into his mouth, gumming it while Art Beaner and his two fellow council members leaned in to confab.

Before John had left the room, they had offered him the job, telling him he could begin ASAP.

Not one to piddle around, he'd accepted. He'd given his notice to the middle school the next day, and as fast as he could pack, he'd moved into the tiny third-floor apartment in the Historical Society's storefront building on Main Street in River Bend.

That was about a week ago.

Before he'd unpacked his bags, John had plunged

into the mess of records left behind by Ms. Dupree—a pack rat if ever there was one—finding a wide array of projects she'd been in the midst of but had never concluded. One in particular had caught his attention: *The Folklore and Legends of River Bend,* which included stories of the frightening dragon-like Piasa Bird and the tale of Jacques Lerner's purported treasure.

John understood that his predecessor had intended to publish a book, but that wasn't his goal. He was more intent on discovery. So he'd already begun gathering as much information as was available in the cluttered Historical Society office: the photographs and diaries left to the Society by River Bend residents; interviews going back several generations; all matter of paper ephemera, including maps, scrapbooks, letters, pamphlets, and postcards.

He had finally found his dream gig, and it wasn't teaching apathetic teenagers. He could already envision the acclaim it would bring him discovering a piece of history that had been only myth.

John pushed aside thoughts of his good fortune, tramping through soggy weeds and brush, batting away branches as he made his way toward the dilapidated cabin in the woods. This, he realized, was about as close to being Indiana Jones as he was going to get.

Blackbirds cackled in the tree above him and darted off in a dark cloud, and John paused, his breath catching—for there was the cabin, dead ahead. From afar it looked solid enough, amazingly so for having withstood the test of time—in this case, several hundred years.

As John walked nearer, he realized the roof badly sagged, and the single window gaped like an open wound without a sign of the sliding boards that surely had once shuttered it. Though the heavy planks composing the front door remained, they looked weather-beaten.

There was an otherworldly quality about the place, particularly with the vague gray of valley fog still stubbornly surrounding it.

John could think of only one word to describe it: *beautiful.*

His heart thumped like a galloping Clydesdale as he approached the ramshackle structure. Despite the tug of weedy slush beneath his boots, he picked up his pace. It wasn't until he was nearly at the threshold of the rotting front door that he thought he glimpsed a pale specter passing through the trees beyond the cabin.

He stopped in his tracks. The hair at his neck bristled.

Was that Jacques Lerner's ghost?

"Hello?" he called out, his voice anxious. "Is someone there?"

The part of John that wasn't like Indiana Jones, which was pretty much all of him save his official fedora, wanted to turn tail and flee. But instead he swallowed hard and slowly pulled the hammer from the pocket of his cargo pants. He'd brought it along to pry up the floorboards if someone hadn't already beaten him to it.

Gathering up his nerve, John called out, "Whoever you are, show yourself!"

He tightly gripped the hammer at his side, ready to raise it and swing at a moment's notice. He walked the perimeter of the cabin, taking slow, even steps. But he saw nothing beyond ethereal patches of sunlight filtered through the heavy boughs above.

Birds squawked. Water burbled. Twigs snapped beneath his feet.

It was okay. He sighed.

He was blessedly alone.

"You've got an overactive imagination, sweetie pie," was what his mother used to tell him when he made up stories about finding treasure in the backyard, and he laughed at himself, believing she was right.

*Nothing to be afraid of,* he thought. Despite the reassurance, a trickle of sweat ran down his back.

But he felt more confident now as he approached the splintered front door. As he tugged it open, it let out a mournful cry.

He took a step inside and had to pause.

The place was small, no bigger than a twelve-by-twelve-foot square, pretty standard for an early nineteenth-century cabin. The puncheon floors beneath his boots looked heavily worn, but he could spot no areas of rot or signs that someone before him had tried to pull them up.

There was a loft overhead, which John surmised Lerner had used to store foodstuffs or to stack the pelts he traded. Not much remained of the wattle-and-daub chimney, save the hole cut in the roof and the piles of twigs and earth used in the construction.

But the stone hearth remained intact, and John imagined the Frenchman kneeling upon it to cook his meals. For surely a fur trader had eaten well enough considering he had no use for the innards of the animals he trapped except to cook them.

Dust motes swam across air thick with the smell of decay. There was a smattering of empty bottles and crushed beer cans, along with cigarette butts and other detritus that confirmed the cabin had hosted a few parties since Jacques Lerner's day.

He could see no useful furniture. He'd bet that anything worth a few cents had been taken long ago. But what John was looking for were things he couldn't see. Surely a man who'd once lived alone in the woods—one as wily as a fur trapper—would have hidden his valuables. Settlers didn't tend to show off as folks did these days.

He figured Jacques Lerner would have dug a spot somewhere outside to bury his gold and any valuable trinkets. Or perhaps shoved them somewhere beneath the old floor, which was where John would begin his hunt.

With a grunt, John got down on his knees. He cocked his hat back on his head and untied the kerchief around his neck, using it to blot the sweat from his brow. Then he retied the bandanna, picked up his hammer, and got to work.

It didn't take long for him to realize that prying up floors made from thick hand-hewn lumber wasn't as easy as he'd imagined. Someone—probably well after Lerner—had used nails to secure the wood, and it seemed from their resistance that they had to be the size of ties on train tracks.

After an hour's work with little to prove for it, John tossed the hammer across the cabin, cursing as he got up from the floor, brushing dirt and leaves from the knees of his pants. He started for the door to get a breath of fresh air and flung it open to find himself staring into the wild eyes of an apparition.

## Chapter 12

IT TOOK LESS than twenty minutes after Betty Winston had left his office for Sheriff Frank Biddle to round up River Bend's volunteer deputies.

He likened them to a handful of mixed nuts, or maybe to Robin Hood's misfit crew of Merry Men, although Frank supposed he should think of them as Merry People in this politically correct day and age.

There was lanky Art Beaner, the chairman of the town council, taking his place beside the portly Henry Potter, who ran a plumbing service out of River Bend (and had recently spearheaded replacement of the town's aging sewer system). Beaner had been a high school wrestler and Eagle Scout, while Henry had served a stint in the army after college, which Frank felt qualified them both for temporary duty on an as-needed basis, usually during flooding—when residents occasionally had to be rescued by canoe—or for traffic control during the town's annual summer carnival.

It wasn't like he'd ever sic them on a terrorist cell or any of the FBI's Ten Most Wanted—not that even he had experience with such tasks. Besides, the men were longtime hunters. Art's coonhound and Henry's Chesapeake Bay retriever were trained to track game. Frank figured it wouldn't hurt to have them try their hand at tracking a human.

After arming the men with walkie-talkies and instructing them to touch base every thirty minutes, Frank sent the pair up to the Winstons' cottage, where Betty would give them some of Bernie's dirty laundry to sniff.

That left Frank to deal with his third and final volunteer deputy.

Since Sarah frowned upon him acting biased against women, he'd tried hard to recruit a female to join the volunteer ranks, and he'd eventually found one: Luann Dupree. Yep, the former director of the Historical Society had once been part of Frank's motley crew. She wasn't ex-military, but Sarah had mentioned Luann had taken self-defense classes when she'd lived in the city. When Frank had questioned Luann's qualifications, she'd given him a demonstration of her skills, catching him behind his heel and flipping him onto his back. (In his defense, her passion for old things and penchant for high heels had not exactly screamed "ass kicker.")

But with Luann gone, ostensibly traveling the country with her online Romeo, he was short one volunteer, and he liked to have three: two to pair up and another to tag along with him. That had led to Frank doing something he figured he'd eventually regret: he'd agreed to let Helen Evans take Luann's place. Even if he hadn't, he realized she'd stick to him like glue until Bernie Winston was located. Mrs. Evans might be a widowed grandmother of five and a septuagenarian, but she was annoyingly persistent and as sharp a tack as anyone Frank had ever met. Frank had bumped heads with Helen enough in the past that he figured it would serve him well to keep her near instead of letting her run her own course.

If there was one thing Frank had learned since he'd become sheriff of River Bend, it was that Mrs. Evans had a tendency to get herself involved in anything and everything that went on in town. If she didn't know all two hundred residents by sight, she at least knew their names and a host of other tidbits about them. Frank had come to think of her a bit as the town crier.

And it was thanks to Mrs. Evans's big mouth—er, her propensity to engage the local community—that he found an additional two dozen townsfolk gathered on the sidewalk in front of his office by the time he'd mapped out to his volunteer deputies the terrain they would cover in their foot search for Bernie Winston. And it would be a foot search because the sheriff figured old Bernie couldn't go far, being that he was eighty-one, suffered from dementia, and had bilateral hip replacements.

"Shouldn't we get going?" Helen Evans asked after Art and Henry had departed, their dogs straining on their leads. "Betty's probably climbing the walls since you told her to go sit at home in case Bernie showed up. She's got Clara with her, and Ellen's back from St. Louis with Sawyer, but I'm sure all she's doing is imagining the worst. Just think how you'd feel if Sarah went missing."

Frank did appreciate when his wife disappeared to her mother's house in Springfield, Illinois, for a few days now and then. But it wasn't like he didn't know where she was. And if he did forget, Sarah called morning, noon, and night to remind him.

Still, Mrs. Evans had a point.

"Yes, ma'am, I'm ready," the sheriff said and sighed, wondering who exactly was in charge of this rodeo.

"Do I get to wear a badge?" she asked, cocking her gray head, and Frank detected a twinkle in her blue eyes despite the serious look on her face.

"No, you don't get a badge," he told her, scowling. "Let's move out," he said and shepherded his sidekick through the door to where the crowd had gathered. They all had on boots of some kind, from rain boots to waders, as Main Street sat a couple inches underwater. Every time a vehicle drove through it, the wake splashed brown puddles onto the sidewalk. In spots, trees that sprouted from green spots between the concrete looked like they were floating, their roots invisible below the brown muck.

So far the sandbags were keeping the water out of the buildings, but it was only a matter of time. If the river didn't start to recede soon, the sandbags would be useless.

Frank cleared his throat and addressed the crowd with a curt "Good morning, all, and thank you for helping out. This is a rescue mission, and time is of the essence."

He spotted more than a few faces that were all too familiar: Ida Bell and Dorothy Feeny, a pair of local tree huggers who looked dressed for a safari; Felicity Timmons, resident green thumb, wearing an oversized hat and traditional black English Wellies; and even shy Mary Garrett from the Cut 'n' Curl in bright purple ankle boots and bedazzled blue jeans, her brown ponytail bobbing.

"I know Mrs. Winston is grateful that you've come out to look for her husband," he announced as his gaze scanned the crowd of mostly weathered faces. "All I ask is that you keep your eyes and ears open. Don't try to cross the creek at any point. Look out for snakes. And avoid taking risks, you hear me?"

He quickly split the two dozen into six groups of four, sending each to canvass a portion of River Bend. The town wasn't big, about a mile square of valley between the bluffs on either side, and with all these hands on deck, Frank had high hopes that Bernie would be found quickly.

"Stick together and stay within the town proper,"

he advised the civilians, because he didn't want to lose one of them in the process of locating Winston. "You may scan the flooded valley and harbor, but do not attempt a rescue or recovery without the proper gear. Leave the deep woods and the bluffs to me and my deputies."

Frank couldn't imagine that Bernie Winston would try to climb the bluffs. It was quite a hike up, and the old man surely didn't have the stamina.

He'd parked his cruiser right on Main Street in the floodwater. It still wasn't more than shin-high, so the undercarriage of his car stayed dry so long as he drove slowly.

"We'll head up Springfield Avenue," he told Helen as they slogged toward the car and got inside, not bothering to shake off wet boots before buckling up. "Since the Winstons live that way, I want to follow the creek beyond the dead end."

The sheriff had instructed Art and Henry to take their dogs up Jersey Avenue to check the back road beyond the edge of town. If Bernie had wandered that way and stuck to the asphalt, he'd end up in farmland. Biddle knew the couple who owned the fields beyond the forest: Hannah and Peter Allen. He'd called them already and given them a heads-up. If Bernie should get that far, they'd let him know.

Biddle drove at a relative snail's pace, and not just because of the twenty-mile-per-hour speed limit. There was enough floodwater that most of the streets looked brown. He spotted at least two canoes tied up to porch railings, preparing for the worst.

He rolled his window down, and Helen did the same, and both kept their eyes peeled for any sign of the missing man. Every now and again Helen would see folks on the sidewalk and would wave them down, calling out, "Bernie Winston's gone missing! If you see him, please, take him home to Betty. She's beside herself."

"Will do, Helen!" they'd call back, and Frank would shake his head.

Yep, he silently affirmed, she was River Bend's town crier, all right, a veritable Silver Alert unto herself.

## Chapter 13

"SHOULDN'T WE STOP at Betty's first and check in?"
Helen asked as Frank Biddle steered the cruiser past
her own whitewashed house on Jersey and slowly—but
slowly—crossed through floodwaters over the bridge
onto Springfield Avenue. "What if she's remembered
something or found a clue that might lead us to Bernie?"

"It'll just delay us."

"I'll pop in and out. It won't take a minute," Helen
promised.

The sheriff sighed before reluctantly agreeing. "Okay,
we'll stop. Though I figure Mrs. Winston would've hollered if she had any brainstorms about where Bernie
might have gone. That's what phones are for."

Maybe so, Helen thought, but sometimes things were
forgotten when one was flustered. "You might as well
park nearby," she suggested, as the Winstons' place sat

beyond a second bridge on a cul-de-sac at Springfield's end. "It'll be best to go by foot from there anyhow."

Biddle gave her a sideways glance that looked anything but pleased. "So you're planning this mission now, are you?"

"I'm only trying to help." Helen knew it didn't pay to knock heads with the sheriff. So she added to appease him, "I'll be quick and then we can search the woods."

"I'll give you exactly what you asked for: one minute," the sheriff said, emphasizing those last two words. "If you're still piddling around and a minute has passed, I'm starting without you."

Helen raised her eyebrows.

So much for the buddy system, eh?

"You won't need to do that."

*My, aren't we crabby,* she thought. Was his foul mood caused by the flood, the missing man, or his wife's failure to believe that her childhood pal had forsaken their friendship for an Internet Romeo? Or was he merely grumpy because he'd miss his usual lunch at the diner? Everyone in River Bend knew how much the sheriff liked the midday meat loaf special.

Heck, everyone out searching for Bernie probably had grumbling bellies. But they could all sit down and eat when Bernie was safe and sound, couldn't they? Maybe hunger would drive them to find the man post-haste.

"Have no fear, Sheriff," she said, reassuring him. "I'll fly in and out of Betty's faster than a toupee in a tornado."

Helen put her hand on the clasp of her seat belt, ready to leap out as soon as he stopped the car. She was raring to go. She'd exchanged her frog rain boots for the waterproof hiking boots she always wore for Ida Bell's spring bird-watching walks, and she cradled a small knapsack in her lap.

Biddle seemed to be eyeing the latter.

"First things first," he said as he shifted his foot from gas to brake. "You've got your walkie in case we get separated while we're hiking?"

"Check," she said, tapping the backpack. "Plus, I've got bottled water, two granola bars, my cell phone, and a first-aid kit."

His thick brows arched. "You could've been a Boy Scout."

"Well, I was married to one for fifty years," she replied with a laugh.

The sheriff summoned up a tight smile.

The upper part of Springfield was dry enough that Helen heard the gravel crunch beneath the tires as he pulled the squad car to the shoulder. It stopped in front of the Winstons' clapboard house with the covered front porch.

Such a pretty place, Helen thought, though it could use a new coat of paint.

She had always liked the fact that the homes in River Bend were mostly Victorian cottages with gabled roofs and carved bargeboard. All had porches and many extended around the entire house. More often than not they were screened in so residents could enjoy mornings and dusk in nice weather without constantly swatting away the bugs.

It was too bad that none of the Winstons' neighbors had been sitting on their front porches drinking coffee in the wee hours when Bernie wandered off. If they had, he never would have gotten far. They would have insisted he step inside and share a mug. Then they would have walked him back home and handed him off to Betty.

It didn't just take a village to raise a child, Helen mused. It took a village to ensure the safety of a confused old man.

"Be right back," she told Biddle as soon as he cut the car's engine.

She slipped her backpack over her shoulder and hopped out, then crossed the front walk and hurried up the porch steps. She hadn't even raised a fist to knock when the door came open.

Clara stood in the threshold, wild-eyed.

"So what's the word? Has he been found? Is he all right?" she asked, rubbing her hands on the thighs of her daisy-covered muumuu.

"Not so fast," Helen told her friend, and she was sorry she didn't have better news. "The search has only begun."

"Yes, yes, I know you're right. Art and Henry were just by with the dogs not fifteen minutes back." Clara bobbed her head. "Betty gave them a dirty old pair of Bernie's jeans to sniff. Good thing she'd missed them doing the laundry this morning."

"The sheriff and I are about to head into the woods toward Lerner's cabin," Helen said. She reached out to take Clara's restless hands and still them. "We'll catch up to him."

"Yes, Lerner's cabin," Clara repeated. "Bernie always did find fascination with that old shack. He trekked there with Sawyer every summer when she was little before the Alzheimer's."

"Have faith," Helen told her, squeezing her hands before letting go.

Clara swallowed hard, glancing over her shoulder. "I'd best get back to Betty. She's a nervous wreck, as you can imagine, though it helps that Ellen's here now. She's such a godsend. I'm not sure what Betty would do without her."

The sheriff loudly cleared his throat from the sidewalk.

"I've got to go," Helen said. She leaned in toward her friend. "He will turn up, and all will be well."

"All will be the same, you mean, which isn't very well at all," Clara whispered. "But I guess it's better than the alternative, isn't it?"

Helen thought she caught a flicker of fear in Clara's eyes before she stepped inside and shut the door.

"Mrs. Evans?"

Though he didn't bark, the sheriff's voice was crisp enough to remind her that this wasn't a social call. She needed to stay on target.

"Coming!" She turned on a boot heel and headed down the porch steps toward Biddle.

He gave her a look. "Did you get anything?"

"I did. Lerner's cabin was somewhere Bernie knew well, so I think we're heading in the right direction," she said and tugged on the straps of her backpack. Without missing a beat, she started walking at a brisk pace. "Last one to the woods is a rotten egg," she called over her shoulder.

He grunted, and his belt jangled as he tried to keep up with her.

When the streets weren't flooded, Helen walked to and from the river every morning—and around town as much as possible—so she was in pretty good shape for a woman her age, if she said so herself. She might have a few decades on the sheriff, but he hardly went anywhere on foot, probably why he was huffing and puffing by the time they reached the dead end of the street and headed into the woods that made up most of the rear end of the valley.

"You seem to . . . know where you're . . . going," the sheriff said between breaths, following her as she crunched over twigs and dead leaves.

"I do," she replied. "And I believe that if I were lost in this thicket, I'd follow the creek, or as close as one can get when it's flooded."

"But what if Bernie . . . isn't thinking . . . logically," Biddle countered.

"I'm sure he's not," Helen told him over her shoulder. "But sometimes it's not logic that guides us. It's instinct. If Bernie trekked to that old cabin time and again with his granddaughter every summer as she grew up, his feet will remember it's there, even if his brain doesn't."

The sheriff huffed and puffed in response.

"Things can't have changed much since I hiked this path with my own children ages ago," she said, feeling like her feet knew exactly what route to take.

Who in River Bend hadn't gone through the woods to Lerner's cabin when it was the focus of half the town's ghost stories? Back when she was a young mother, it had been simple enough to walk in the creek bed during the heat of the summer. They'd picked up uncountable rocks along the way, cracking them open to see if they sparkled on the inside. "Look, Mommy, a geode!" she could hear a young voice gleefully cry. Occasionally, they'd turned up fossils. But that was when the creek had been dry as a bone.

As Helen pressed on, tree branches with budding leaves stretched their arms wide in front of her, as did the thick boughs of evergreens. She ducked when need be, scrabbling toward the noise of the water because it was the water that would lead them. Without the creek, there were just trees and more trees. If you blindly wended your way through, you'd end up either climbing the bluff or hiking out of the valley into the farmland beyond.

If only the flooding hadn't turned the creek bed into a raging river and the banks on either side into a swamp.

The best-laid plans and all that.

Helen realized they'd have to steer clear of the bog the flood had created, sticking to the tree line to avoid the water.

"If you . . . want to . . . hang back," Biddle puffed, catching up with her, "it's . . . okay. I can . . . continue to search . . . on my own."

Helen looked back at him and smiled. He was standing with hands on his knees, catching his breath. "I was going to tell you the same thing," she quipped.

She had given birth four times, had nursed her beloved husband back from one heart attack, and had watched another take his life. She was hardly going to let a little thing like water thwart her. The best tool she could utilize to plow through the brush was her patience, and *that* she had in spades . . . though she couldn't say the same for Frank Biddle.

He scowled as he straightened up. He set his hands on his hips, on either side of his rounded belly, and Helen saw him open his mouth to respond. Only nothing emerged.

Instead from somewhere deeper in the woods came a terrified shriek.

Biddle's eyes widened at the sound. "Was that a hawk?" he asked. "Or maybe an eagle?"

Having lived in the valley for half a century, Helen

had heard plenty of squawks and calls and cries of birds of prey, but that scream wasn't one of them.

*"Bernie?"* she found herself saying, her heart thumping in her chest. Her legs started moving even as she prodded, "Time to shake a leg, Sheriff!"

## Chapter 14

JOHN SCREAMED AGAIN as he saw the pale specter of a man standing in the doorway, his skeletal frame haloed by the daylight. He felt a trickle of damp begin to run down his leg, but he was too petrified to care. "You . . . You're Jacques Lerner's . . . g-ghost," he stammered, his whole arm shaking as he raised it to point.

"I am?" the apparition moaned.

He was gaunt, his eyes filmy, white hair in disarray, his face scratched. His blue shirt was streaked with dirt, and his pants were wet up to his shins. If he wasn't a ghost, he was the walking dead.

"You're not real! You can't be!" John cried and made a dash for freedom, knocking into a bony shoulder as he rushed past the specter. His boot caught on a root that had grown up through the wooden steps, and he tripped, hitting the ground with a *thud* and biting his tongue.

"I—I'm not real?" the ghost repeated from behind him. The voice sounded strained, stuttering as he asked, "I-Is this your house? I don't know where I am. I was looking for the coal mine, but I think I got lost. I'm an engineer for Peabody."

*An engineer for Peabody?*

Did the ghosts of French fur traders say things like that?

Deliberately, John picked himself up and turned around, willing his racing heart to slow down. He wrinkled his brow and took a good, long look at his ghost.

Could he see through him?

*No.*

Was he floating off the ground?

*No.*

Oh, geez, he wasn't a ghost, he realized, just a tired old man, clearly lost.

As the staccato pace of his pulse eased, John studied the withered face.

He didn't know the guy from Adam—had no clue what coal mine he was babbling about, although there were plenty of caves in the area—but he sure as shooting wasn't a zombie or the specter of Jacques Lerner come to chase away a treasure hunter. He was flesh and bones. Well, mostly bones, from the gaunt look of him.

"I'm so sorry. I'm a fool with a vivid imagination,"

John said and stood up, though his knees wobbled. He squared his shoulders, dusting himself off. "I tend to get carried away sometimes."

The fellow gave him a blank stare.

"You know, I don't think there's a coal mine in this particular valley," John said and approached the stranger, this time without trepidation. "You're quite a bit off the beaten path. Do you live in River Bend?"

The man got the most puzzled look on his face. "My wife and I, we're from Coal City. Is that near? I seem to have lost all sense of direction. I've been traveling a lot lately. That must be it."

"What's your name?" John tried asking. He sensed something wasn't right, and it went beyond the man's frazzled appearance. He could see it in his eyes. They had a fuzzy, vacant look to them. "Do you know who you are?"

"Win. My name's Win, at least that's what my buddies call me," the man replied, then made a face, like that wasn't quite right. After a slight hesitation, he explained, "I work for Peabody, inspecting the mines." He scratched at his chin, his befuddled gaze raking in the woods around them. "I must be lost."

No fooling.

John sighed, relaxing. The fellow might not be a real ghost, but he was definitely the ghost of a man and lost in more ways than one. He could see all the signs.

"So your name's Win," John repeated. "Is that your first name or your last name?"

The fellow had to stop and think. "Winston," he finally said. "It's Winston."

John wondered if the old guy's mother had been a fan of Churchill.

"I need . . . I need to . . ." He cocked his head, white hair flying about his crown like Einstein on a bad day. "I need to find my wife. I should get home . . . Gotta clean up before the cocktail party."

*Cocktail party?*

Who this guy was, John hadn't a clue; but he hardly knew everyone in town. He'd been living there only a matter of weeks, just long enough to have met a handful of residents. It wasn't as though he were there to make friends, besides. John was in River Bend to do a job, nothing more, nothing less.

"Do you know where you live?" he asked.

"A house . . . We have a house," Winston said. "It's painted yellow, bright yellow. It's near the library in Coal City," he said, but he sounded very unsure. "Betty's sister, she came to stay with us for a while, but I can't recall her name."

Oh, boy.

If the man was from Coal City, then he'd been wandering for days. If John's memory served, Coal City was a small town that sat about an hour south of Chicago. He remembered seeing the exits en route to a conference in the Windy City. That put it about three or four hours from River Bend.

"Are you sure you aren't from River Bend?"

"I don't think . . . ," he started, before he paused and shook his head. "I don't know."

"It's okay." John sucked in his cheeks as he gazed longingly over Winston's shoulder at the centuries-old cabin. He itched like mad to get back inside and resume his attempt to pry up the floorboards. But he couldn't very well rip apart Jacques Lerner's historic abode while this Winston fellow stood and watched, even if the old guy was addled.

No, he had to be cautious. If he screwed up this gig, it meant giving up everything. What if he carried on and Winston had a moment lucid enough to tattle on him back in River Bend? The town council would surely fire him in an instant, and then everything he'd done to get here would be for nothing.

So John sucked in a deep breath and put his exploring on hold.

"How about this," he said, setting his hands on his hips. "Let's take a walk and get you back to town. I'm sure your family's been wondering where you are."

"My family? It's just me and my wife. There's no one else," Winston said in a sandpaper voice. "She's a gem, she is. I'd do anything for her. Her name is—" He stared off into the trees, blinking rapidly. "It's Betty. Yes, Betty. She'll be looking for me. We have a cocktail party to attend."

"Right, the cocktail party," John said, because he knew it was best to just play along. It wasn't like you could argue with dementia and win. "All right, Win-

ston. You can lean on me, and I'll get you back to town."
He walked up to the man and took his arm.

"That's kind of you," he said with a vacant smile. "I
do feel a bit weak."

With one last lustful look at the cabin, John started
back the same way he'd come, far more slowly with the
old man at his elbow. They weren't even halfway to the
edge of the woods and to the dead end of Springfield
Avenue when John heard the sounds of snapping twigs
and a woman's voice calling out, "Shake a leg, Sheriff!"

*Sheriff?*

John panicked. They were definitely out looking for
the old guy. For a second he thought about dumping
Winston and running for cover.

*Hey, calm down,* he told himself. He'd done nothing
wrong, not that Winston had seen, anyhow.

"I hope we still have time before the party. I think
I need to change my clothes," Winston mumbled, and
his chin drooped to his chest, like the guy had nothing
left in him.

John tugged at his hat brim, knowing what he had
to do. He made sure he had a strong arm around him
as they limped along. "It'll be all right," he said aloud.
"We'll get you home to change before the first cocktail
is poured."

The old man nodded.

As they rounded a thicket heavy with invasive
honeysuckle, John caught sight of a gray-haired woman
turned so he could see her purple knapsack. Just beyond

her was the sheriff in his tan uniform, shiny badge at his chest, staring in John's direction with a surprised look on his face.

"Hey there!" he called out to them, his heart thumping as he half dragged a limping Winston forward. "I found this one wandering around the old cabin," he said between breaths. "If either of you knows where he lives, that'd be a big help. He doesn't seem to have a clue, and neither do I."

## Chapter 15

"Is that who I think it is?" Helen said, doing a double take.

She stopped in her tracks, giving Biddle a chance to catch up. She heard him panting beside her, but he said nothing, clearly as dumbfounded as she.

For dead ahead of them was a most odd and interesting sight: two grown men emerging from the woods, one looking very much like Jacob Marley, minus his chains, and the other like a wannabe Indiana Jones, complete with scarf nattily knotted about his neck and the signature dark brown fedora on his head.

The score for an adventure movie swelled in her head.

*Dum-da-dum-dum, dum-da-dum, dum-da-dum-dum, dum-da-dum-dum-dum.*

She breathed softly, "Well, I'll be a monkey's uncle."

Biddle pushed his hat back to wipe at the beads of sweat on his brow. "So, Indiana Jones found Bernie? I guess Spider-Man was busy," he said, getting his wind back before he tugged his walkie-talkie from his utility belt.

"It's John Danielson, the man who took Luann's place," Helen said, even though Biddle surely knew it already. He kept tabs on the comings and goings in River Bend nearly as well as she did.

Biddle nodded as the two men came nearer. "He's a character, all right, and now I think we know which one."

"I just hope I don't slip and call him Indy."

Danielson hadn't been dressed like Indiana Jones when she'd first met him at the Historical Society. He'd appeared more the Dockers-and-button-down type, and he hadn't smiled much that she'd noticed. He'd seemed on the shy side, staring mostly at his shoes when he'd told her and Clara that they could no longer sort photos in the upstairs room. Shortly after, he'd installed them in a small office on the first floor that was little more than a walk-in closet lined with file cabinets. A few days later he'd suspended volunteer work altogether, blaming the floodwaters for his decision. "I don't want anyone taking a risk coming here," he'd insisted.

"Does he realize shin-deep water is nothing compared to '93?" Clara had whispered. "We got around by kayak and canoe . . ."

"Um, Deputies, what's your twenty?"

Helen heard the scratch as Biddle got on the walkie-talkie and connected with Art Beaner and Henry Potter, telling them to cease and desist in the search for Bernie Winston.

"Let the rest of the volunteers know that he's been located and we're bringing him back. Art, can you meet us with your golf cart? The old guy looks pretty wobbly."

"That's a ten-four, Sheriff," Art's voice crackled before the sheriff put the walkie away.

Helen pulled off her knapsack and retrieved a bottle of water, holding on to it as she tramped through the brush after the sheriff, heading toward the pair of men who'd emerged from the thicket and meeting them halfway.

"Here you go," she said, offering her bottle of water to Bernie. "You look awfully dehydrated."

"I am parched. Thank you, ma'am," he said, as if she were a stranger and not the woman who'd been best friends with his sister-in-law for years. He took the bottle in his shaky grip and tipped it between cracked lips. He downed most of it before he stopped and wiped his mouth with the back of his hand. "You seem familiar," he told her. "You must work for Peabody, too? Are you a secretary?"

"Peabody," Helen repeated, because the name didn't click. She glanced at the sheriff, who shrugged.

The Historical Society director tipped back his Indiana Jones hat. "Apparently, Bernie got lost while he was inspecting the coal mines for Peabody. I'm guessing he was an employee a while back."

Ah, he wasn't talking about a *man* named Peabody, but Peabody Energy.

"Oh, he did, indeed, a long time ago," Helen said, because Clara had told her about living with Bernie and Betty in Coal City when Clara was still in high school. Betty and Bernie had taken her in when she'd had trouble with her stepfather. Bernie was a young engineer and traveled frequently for Peabody. Perhaps that was why he'd wandered off. He'd gone back to those days in his addled mind.

"Are you injured, Mr. Winston?" Biddle asked, taking the man's arm and looking him over with a squint. "Do you think you can walk back to Springfield?"

"Springfield, Illinois?" Bernie looked confused.

"No, the street, sir, in River Bend," the sheriff clarified. "Not the city."

But Bernie only got more agitated. "Where's my wife? Is she still in the car? Is she . . . Is she looking for me?"

"She's back at your house with your daughter and granddaughter, and she's very worried about you," Helen said, patting his hand. "Now let's get you home so she can stop worrying. Ellen's there, too."

"Ellen?"

"Your daughter."

He shook his head. "No," he said. "We weren't ever able . . ."

"Let's move it," Frank Biddle said, cutting him off.

Helen stepped aside as the sheriff and John Danielson bookended Bernie and began helping him through the brush.

"The sooner we get back, the sooner Betty and Ellen will be able to breathe again," Helen remarked from behind them.

But Bernie seemed not to have heard her.

No matter. She walked behind the three men, watching as Biddle and the fellow from the Historical Society patiently maneuvered Bernie through the woods, sticking to the dry turf despite the tangled vines and twigs and poison ivy.

She listened to the rise and fall of their voices as Bernie constantly asked where they were and where they were going in a never-ending circular conversation. Twigs snapped underfoot as she followed the men, while nearby the creek sounded noisy, the rising waters rushing by.

Every now and then, the sheriff and John Danielson would pause, allowing Bernie to catch his breath. "Walking hurts so much," Helen caught Bernie saying.

"Your wife said you've had two hip surgeries," Biddle told him. "I guess that would explain it."

"Hip surgeries? I don't know what you're talking about," Bernie replied, sounding grouchy. "I'm fit as a fiddle. Except . . . Except for my bum knee. I hurt it a couple years ago in school during football . . . during practice."

"Right," Biddle said, humoring him. "You think you can keep going, sir? If I could carry you, I would."

"No need . . . no need," Bernie said, defiant. "I'm perfectly fine."

"Okay, then, let's move out, though I'm sorry for dragging you through the brush, but the creek's overflowed . . ."

With every step Helen took on their slow hike back to Springfield Avenue, she felt more and more sympathy for Betty Winston. She thought of the hours and days and months she'd dealt with Joe and his crabby demeanor as he'd recovered from his first heart attack and the surgery that had ensued. She decided that she'd had it easy compared to Betty.

"We're almost there," John Danielson piped up as they came out of the woods and into the clearing just behind the houses on the cul-de-sac.

As they trudged toward the asphalt, Helen saw a crowd of a dozen or so neighbors gathered.

"Bring him here, Sheriff!" Art Beaner called from his golf cart. His coonhound sat, panting, in the rear-facing seat. "I'll get him the rest of the way home."

John Danielson hung back as Art hopped out of the cart and helped the sheriff guide Bernie to the vehicle. Helen watched as he pulled his brown fedora low over his forehead and faded back, like he didn't want the attention.

Helen made her way over to him, catching him before he took off. "Thank you, Mr. Danielson," she said. "For finding Bernie while you were out in the woods, um . . ."

"Hiking," he quickly filled in for her. "I like getting into nature when the weather's nice, and I wanted to see Lerner's cabin. It's such a strong piece of local folklore."

"Well, thank goodness you were there," Helen went on. "The place is lodged in Bernie's memory, so it must have drawn him. But if no one had been around, who knows how long he might've wandered and what could have happened to him."

"I'm glad to help," Danielson told her and finally met her eyes. "Like so many people these days, I have family with dementia, so I'm sympathetic. Now I should be off, ma'am."

"Of course," Helen said, her gaze on Danielson's back as he lumbered away, crossing to the far side of the cul-de-sac and climbing into a black SUV.

Then she turned her attention to Bernie, now surrounded by well-wishers.

"What's the fuss about?" he asked as his neighbors hovered, telling him how lucky he was and how thankful they were for his return. "Is this a parade?"

"Yeah, Mr. Winston, it's a parade," the sheriff told him.

"What for?"

"For you," Biddle said. Then he patted the roof of the cart, and Beaner nodded, driving Bernie down the road.

Helen let out a held breath.

"Okay, folks, everyone head on home," Biddle said loudly. "Mr. Winston needs to be with his family."

The crowd began to disperse.

Helen watched the sheriff gesture, shooing everyone

on their way. Then he got on his phone, nodding as he spoke, before he put his phone away.

He glanced back at her, giving a jerk of his chin, and she caught up to him as he walked toward his black-and-white. "I've got Doc Melville heading to the Winstons' place now. He's going to check out the old man, see if he needs further medical attention. Doc said if he's dehydrated enough, he might need an IV."

"Good thinking," she told him.

He grunted. "You need a lift home?"

"No, I'm fine." At his raised eyebrows she pointed down to her boots. "I can wade through the water on Jersey. It's only ankle-deep."

"If you're sure . . ."

"I'm sure."

He tipped his hat to her before opening his door and getting inside.

Helen stood by as he drove off, crunching gravel beneath his tires. She started her walk home, an absent smile on her face. She was so glad they'd found Bernie, and he seemed to be in good shape. That was some-thing, right?

As she neared the Winstons' house, she spotted Doc Melville's car arriving. The dusty sedan pulled up smack in front and parked with a squeal of old brakes. Amos Melville emerged from the passenger's side, his medical bag in hand. He was up the front walk and to the porch before Helen could call out to him.

Doc's wife, Fanny, came out of the driver's side and

slammed shut the door as she looked over at Helen. "Heck of a way to start the week, eh?" she said. A broad smile took shape beneath a bulbous nose. Below a fringe of short bangs her eyes twinkled.

Helen smiled. "At least this story has a happy ending," she remarked, walking toward Fanny and closing the gap between them.

"How'd it feel to play Girl Scout?" Doc's wife asked.

Helen scratched her age-speckled arm. "I think a few mosquitoes made a meal of me, but otherwise I'm just fine."

"I hope Bernie's all right."

"He seemed to be faring pretty well physically," Helen said, hesitating. "But he's awfully out of it."

"That's how Alzheimer's works."

Helen looked up at the house. "Maybe I should go inside. I could check on Clara and see if they need me to bring lunch. Or if Sawyer's there with Ellen, I could take her somewhere to occupy her time."

"Like the underwater playground?" Fanny said sarcastically.

Helen winced. "You're right. Maybe the library . . ."

"Water's gotten past the sandbags and the carpet's wet. They'll have to rip it all out. It closed in the meantime."

"Oh, dear."

"You should go home," Fanny told her and wrapped an arm around her. "You've done enough this morning. You look tired, and I'd imagine your muscles weren't too thrilled at tramping through the woods. Maybe you should lie down for a while and nap."

Helen nodded. "You're right. I am tired."

"You want me to walk with you?" Fanny asked. "I'll lend you an arm if you'd like."

But Helen glanced at her friend's feet. She had on pristine white tennis shoes. "You'll only ruin your Keds."

"I can buy a new pair."

"I'll be fine," she said, giving Fanny's arm a squeeze as it came off her shoulders. "Call me later, will you, please? Let me know how Bernie checks out."

"I will," Fanny assured her. "Amos has tried to convince Betty to place him in assisted living before, but she resisted. Maybe now she'll change her mind."

"Maybe."

Before she headed off, Helen turned back toward the Winstons' house. She caught sight of a face in the window, the ghost of a man with dark eyes and wild white hair. He appeared lost even then, looking for a way out.

Sadness swept through her.

She lifted a hand to wave, held it there for a moment. But he didn't act like he'd seen her. Then as abruptly as he'd appeared, he was gone.

## Chapter 16

JACKSON LEE HAD borrowed a pickup truck from his buddy the used-car dealer in Jerseyville, who owed him more on a poker debt than a Cartier pen paid off. He would have driven his Caddy except it sat too low to the ground. He didn't want to take a chance that the flood-waters would drown his old DeVille when he hit Main Street. He figured it wouldn't hurt to switch vehicles anyhow, considering he planned a quick trip back to the old Victorian on Springfield Avenue where Bernie Winston lived.

Jackson wanted to get paid on that contract Bernie had signed, and he was itching to grab a paycheck before Bernie went boots-up or got committed, which-ever came first. Not to mention the fact that he'd left his flashy Cartier Roadster ballpoint at the Winstons' place when he'd bolted a few weeks before. It was his lucky pen and the nicest one he'd ever owned. He'd been back a few times late at night, sitting out front and trying to figure out a way in. If he had to sneak through a window to get that sucker back, he'd do it. But maybe he could catch Bernie alone again . . .

"Uh-oh," he said under his breath and slowed to a crawl as he approached the house.

He spotted the sheriff's black-and-white parked out front. A golf cart with a dog riding shotgun was just pulling out of the Winstons' driveway, and crowds of people milling about began to drift past him.

What the heck was going on?

Jackson stopped one house shy of the Winstons' and rolled down his window. "What's up? Is everything okay?" he asked a woman in hip-high waders. She looked ready for some trout fishing.

"Better than okay! He's been found," she trilled, and a crooked smile scrunched up her birdlike features. "Bernie's safe and sound."

"Thank goodness," Jack replied, because it seemed a sure bet.

"Sheriff doesn't want anyone hanging around, bothering the family, though." The woman scratched her beaked nose. "Doc's going to check him out, and then they'll need time alone. So you might as well scoot."

"Of course," he murmured. "Thanks for the heads-up."

"You're welcome," she said as he paused. Then she headed off with a smaller woman trotting behind her shouting, "Ida, wait for me!"

Jackson was sure he'd seen them both before, but he couldn't conjure up their names to save his life. There were so many hens living in this tiny burg that one looked a lot like the next. He usually stayed away from the women, besides. They were way too suspicious. It was one reason he liked to do business on the golf course. No nosy wives around to keep their husbands from sealing the deal with a handshake.

Jackson peered ahead at the Winstons' porch and saw the sheriff with an arm around a rail-thin man who shakily ascended the steps. Soon a distraught-looking woman appeared at the front door. Her sharp features seemed to contort beneath the cap of her white hair.

He recognized *that* hen well enough.

Jack's eyes narrowed.

If she was Bernie Winston's harpy wife, was that pathetic-looking fellow Bernie?

*Wow.*

The old guy hadn't exactly looked all peaches and cream the last time Jackson had seen him. But now he was even gaunter and dirty, to boot, like he'd been dragged through the mud and back again. So he'd wandered off and gotten lost in the woods, had he? Things were progressing faster than Jackson had realized.

*Confound it,* he thought with a shake of his head, taking in the scene. He wasn't going to get a check from Bernie today, not with the sheriff hanging around, and he for damned sure wasn't going to get his Cartier ballpoint back.

He'd just have to come back when things were quieter.

Rather than risk Bernie's wife catching sight of him, Jackson rolled up his window and drove off, heading to the diner. If anyone could fill him in on the day's events, it was Erma.

There were a couple of other trucks parked out front in the shin-high water. Jack was glad he'd worn a pair of beat-up Lucchese boots, 'cause he was about to get them wet. Though he wasn't thrilled about wading to the sidewalk, he tugged up his trousers and went. He splashed through puddles to the diner's door and pulled it wide. As a bell jingled overhead, he stamped the water from his boots on the already-soggy doormat.

The place was quieter than it normally was, and Jack wasn't sure if that was because of the flood or because a good chunk of the population seemed to be congregated in front of Bernie Winston's house.

As soon as Erma saw him, she motioned him toward a booth near the window.

"What's all the fuss about Bernie Winston?" he asked her point-blank.

"The fuss? You mean him disappearing for half a day and turning up near Lerner's cabin?" she said, her eyes bright above the folds in her cheeks. "Henry Potter was just by and said he got word on his walkie-talkie that Bernie came out of the thicket alive. Councilman Beaner headed off in his golf cart to go pick him up. Poor old guy."

"So he got out of the house on his lonesome?" Jackson asked. "He isn't locked inside?"

"I guess not. He snuck right past his wife and slipped away," she said, looking surprised that he had to ask. "Mrs. Winston was frantic. The sheriff had to round up a posse to hunt him down. Thank heavens, he was okay. Who knows what could've happened to him if he'd been left out there alone for too long, especially with the water rising as fast as it is. You know how confused those folks get. I'm sure it wouldn't have been a happy ending."

"Uh-hum," Jackson grunted, hoping that would suffice. He didn't want to interrupt the flow of Erma's monologue by talking.

"He's got a bad case of old timer's disease from the sounds of it," she told him and fished around the pocket of her apron. "I'd guess he's getting worse, too, if he's slipping out and disappearing into the backwoods. Probably won't be long till Betty has to put him somewhere for safekeeping."

"Geez, that sounds distressing," he said, and it was the truth. If he didn't work fast, he was going to lose one of his golden egg–laying geese. That was one thing he didn't like about his clients from River Bend: they tended to die off before he was done shaking out their pockets.

"I can't blame Mrs. Winston if she does lock him up somewhere." Erma shrugged. "It's a tough boat to be in. At least the old guy's safe for now, right? One day at a time, that's all you can do." She found her order pad and plucked a pencil from behind her ear. "What'll it be today, hon? A cup of joe and a doughnut?"

"Just the coffee, please."

Erma nodded but seemed in no hurry to leave. "I had an uncle with old timer's," she said and sighed. "It was like he turned back into a baby. By the end he was in diapers. He couldn't feed himself or tie his shoes. It's a sad way to go."

"Any way's a sad way to go," Jack said, because he wasn't sure if losing one's mind was any worse than eating a bad clam or stepping off a curb and getting hit by a bus.

"I'll be back in a tick with your order," Erma told him.

"Thanks."

She gave him a wink then plodded off in her ortho-pedic sneakers.

Jackson slipped his cell phone from his breast pocket and made a note to himself. He had to find a way to get back into Bernie's and snag a check before the old guy was put into lockup at some facility for loony tunes, and he wanted his prized pen back, too. Though he'd have to be careful. If that hawk-nosed wife of Bernie's caught him again, she might actually call the sheriff and have him arrested for real.

He sighed.

Desperate times called for desperate measures, eh? He might have to resort to a little B and E, which he didn't like to do.

When Erma brought his coffee, he barely took a slurp before he glanced at the clock on his phone and realized he'd let the time get away.

If he pushed the pedal to the metal, he could take the back road out of River Bend and get to the Jerseyville Country Club for a twelve-o'clock tee time with a couple of retired gentlemen he'd struck up a conversation with last week at Fran & Marilyn's over the breakfast buffet.

"Time to make the doughnuts," he said to himself.

Then he paid his bill, leaving Erma a five-dollar tip for a cup of joe. Hey, it never hurt to keep the locals friendly, particularly the ones like Erma, who kept a finger on the pulse of this little gold mine of a town.

## Chapter 17

"HELEN, WAKE UP."

The voice worked its way into Helen's dream.

She was gobbling meat loaf and mashed potatoes at the diner with Clara Foley. Clara wore a bright purple muumuu and sat beside a ghostly looking Bernie Winston, who kept whispering, "Water. I need water." All the while Amber perched center table, swishing his tail across their plates until his fur turned soggy with gravy.

"Get up," the voice said again more urgently, this time accompanied by a relentless shaking of her shoulder. "I need your help."

The dream dissolved, leaving fogginess in its wake.

Helen opened her eyes to find Sarah Biddle leaning over the wicker chaise lounge on which she'd fallen asleep. Fanny Melville had been right: she was tired after the hike to find Bernie. She'd gotten back to the house, pulled off her muddy hiking boots, and cleaned up a bit. She'd eaten a granola bar, fed Amber a fresh can of Fancy Feast, and plunked down on the porch.

Her eyes had felt soggy as she tried to work a cross-word puzzle. Then Fanny called to tell her Doc had checked out Bernie and, except for some cuts and bruises and a mild case of dehydration, he was fine.

She'd hung up, feeling tired but satisfied. It hadn't taken but five minutes after removing her glasses and lying down before she'd nodded off. It was too bad that she hadn't locked the screen door before napping.

"If you'd just get up and put on some shoes, we could be off in a flash. This shouldn't take too long," Sarah Biddle was saying.

"Off to where?" Helen asked, sitting up and fumbling for the glasses she'd left on the end table. She rubbed her eyes before propping her specs on the bridge of her nose. "And why on earth should I go with you?"

Hadn't she rendered enough assistance for one day?

"Because you're the only one who hasn't told me I'm crazy thinking Luann's in trouble," Sarah said.

Helen couldn't argue with that.

Instead of taking a chair, the sheriff's wife settled down on the coffee table smack in front of Helen. If her bright eyes and rabid gnawing of her lip were any indi-cation, she was pretty worked up about something.

"Frank's about to kill me, as he can't get into the garage, because that's where I put the boxes of Luann's things," she began to ramble. "I'm not hauling them to storage until I've gone through every piece, and it's taken me these past three weeks, but I found something." She stopped to swallow. "It was wedged between pages 251 and 252 in one of Lu's books."

What on earth was she babbling about?

"It was a sheet from a memo pad with a phone number."

Helen blinked. "Whose number?"

"I'm not exactly sure, if we're talking the grand scheme of things," Sarah said. She fished in the pocket of her windbreaker and pulled out a folded slip of paper. "But it must mean something. It was stuck inside the book about pirate hunters that Lu loved so much, the one she was reading when she started moaning about wanting to have a real-life adventure instead of just living vicariously through old photos and relics from digs. It was about the same time she met Mr. Maybe online."

"You figure it's for him?" Helen took the paper from her and unfolded it. She squinted through her specs at the numbers scribbled on the piece of notepaper with Luann Dupree's embossed monogram.

"Well, I did a quick Google search, and it connected me with an address in Belleville."

"And . . . ?"

Sarah plucked her cell phone from her other pocket and started tapping and scrolling until she found what she was looking for. "It came up as belonging to a woman named Penny Tuttle, age seventy-two."

"So not her Internet Romeo?"

"Maybe she's an expert on old artifacts. What if she's seen whatever it was that Lu thought was so valuable?"

Helen's shoulders sagged. After this morning's frantic search for Bernie, she didn't exactly feel in the mood for chasing down a phone number that Luann left behind in a pirate-hunting book. It sounded like a futile task anyway.

"Why don't you ask Frank to go with you?"

He was the sheriff, after all. Perhaps he could keep his wife from getting into any trouble.

Sarah sniffed. "Frank's dealing with the aftermath of finding Mr. Winston. He has to cancel the Silver Alert and God knows what else, and he's still in charge of sandbagging detail and trying to evacuate folks from low-lying homes around the harbor. They're putting everyone up in Godfrey and Jerseyville until the waters recede."

Helen raised her eyebrows. "So he declined."

Smart fellow.

"I didn't exactly tell him. Instead, I came to you," Sarah said and reached for her hand. "All of River Bend knows how good you are at solving puzzles. Please, come with me, and let's just see if this clue leads to anything. If it doesn't, I promise, I'll let this go. I won't say another word about Lu's taking off. I'll believe that she's doing what she wants to be doing, like the rest of the town, and I'll stick her stuff in storage without a second thought. She can come collect it when she's done gal-livanting around, and I won't waste any more time worrying about her."

Sarah sounded sincere enough, though she didn't look at all happy at the prospect of giving up.

"Can't you please find someone else?"

Helen had planned to bake a casserole to take to Betty Winston, and she had books to return to the library— Oh, wait, hadn't Fanny said it was closed due to flooding? And she didn't have her volunteer gig at the Historical Society anymore, not until the new director decided to let them back in.

"I don't want anyone else to come. I promise, it won't take too long," Sarah said, adding, "Pretty please with sugar on top," in such a desperate way, the same tone Helen's grown children and grandchildren used when they needed something from her.

*Criminy.*

Reluctantly, Helen gave in, which was what she usually ended up doing when one of her brood called begging, as well.

"Okay, I'll go," she said, earning a little whoop from Sarah Biddle. "But only if we stick to my plan," she added and stood.

"Great! Um, what plan?" Sarah looked up from her coffee-table perch.

"When we get to the address, we knock on a door or ring a bell," she said. "If no one answers, we leave. There's to be no funny business, you hear me? No wandering off and poking around where we don't belong."

It was something Helen had done a time or two in the past, so she understood the appeal. But she wasn't as convinced as Sarah that something untoward had happened to Luann Dupree, so she wasn't willing to risk invading a woman's privacy—or worse, getting arrested by the Belleville police—just to placate the sheriff's wife.

"What if we find something fishy?" Sarah protested.

"No, no, no," Helen cut her off with a wag of her finger. "That's the deal. If you can't stick to it, I'm out."

The other woman seemed ready to argue then bit down on her lip. Her shoulders slumped.

"All right," she murmured. But her gaze dropped to somewhere near Helen's feet as she added, "You win. I'll behave." It was only after she'd finished speaking that she lifted her chin to meet Helen's eyes again.

Hardly confidence inspiring, Helen thought and had to wonder if Sarah was crossing her fingers behind her back.

"Let's make this quick," she said, wondering if she'd live to regret it. "Let me find my shoes and my bag, and we can be off."

"Thank you, Helen." Sarah beamed.

"Don't thank me yet," she said, walking toward the French doors that led inside from the porch. "Wait until we're back safe and sound and neither of us is under arrest for trespassing."

It was just two o'clock, Helen realized as she sat down on her bed to pull on her boots. If all went well—or at least not *unwell*—they'd be back in a matter of two and a half to three hours, in plenty of time for her to get a tuna casserole in the oven and take it to the Winstons for dinner.

By the time she'd brushed her hair, put on a bit of lipstick, and grabbed her handbag, Sarah was pacing the porch linoleum impatiently.

"We'll have to take an alternate route, what with the flood closing the ramp off the River Road, but I've got it all mapped out," the woman told her, holding the door open to Helen as she appeared.

The appeal of wide-open spaces must have lured Amber from wherever he'd been hiding. In a flash he zipped around Helen and made a lunge for freedom. Luckily, she spotted his big furry carcass before he could make it past Sarah's legs.

"Oh, no, you don't!" she said and grabbed for him, catching him by his hind feet. "You'll get more than your paws wet outside these days. Don't you know there's a flood?"

Amber let out a howl, but she kept a hold of him until she could reel him back in. She picked him up, despite his wiggling, and deposited him in the living room. Then she shut the French doors so he couldn't get out on the porch while she was away.

"If I'm not back by five o'clock, call the sheriff and tell him his crazy wife has taken me hostage, *capisce*?"

Amber gave her the evil eye and an irritated swish of tail.

Helen locked the French doors for good measure.

## Chapter 18

THEY HAD TO exit River Bend via the back road since the ramp off the highway was flooded. That meant a side trip through Elsah before they could get on the Great River Road and scoot south alongside the swollen Mississippi to Alton. After a few more detours they were on their way to Belleville.

Helen didn't say much. She had the Winston family on her mind. Surely they felt great relief that Bernie was okay. But what would come next? If he'd escaped once, it could happen again. What a terrible spot to be in, she thought, her heart heavy.

". . . so I told Frank you were visiting an old friend with me, and he didn't even ask questions. He's got so much on his mind," Sarah was saying, and Helen tried very hard to shut her out.

She stared out the window at the passing scenery—

mostly brown water as far as she could see—while Sarah began to ruminate again on Luann Dupree's vanishing act.

"My guess is that he targeted Lu somehow, maybe through an online group. I went back through my old e-mails from last year. I found one where Lu mentioned wanting to write a book about River Bend and all the local legends attached to it, like the Piasa Bird, Jacques Lerner, and the connection to Lewis and Clark. Lu found something in an old journal that referred to a stopover when Lewis and Clark were exploring the Mississippi River Valley. Do you think she found real evidence relating to that? Some proof that they'd been in our little village?" the sheriff's wife asked. "If she uncovered physical proof and spilled the beans to someone, it could be why she was targeted. Any antiquity she could tie back to Lewis and Clark would be worth millions to a museum, probably even more to a private collector buying on the black market."

"There's a black market in River Bend?" Helen asked, something Sarah said finally piquing her interest.

"There's a black market everywhere, thanks to the Internet. I did a lot of research online about it," Sarah told her. "Plundering is big business these days and lots of stolen artifacts are ending up on eBay."

Helen thought of the old adage that cheaters never prosper and decided that it was a big fat lie.

"I just need to track down this fake boyfriend of hers. I know he's responsible. It's the only thing that makes sense," Sarah went on, frowning as she drove. "I tried to locate her Facebook page so I could go through her friends list, but it's really gone. If I could pin down her Mr. Maybe, get even a little information on who he is and where he's from, there's a chance I can find him."

"She never told you anything about him?"

Sarah snorted. "I barely knew he existed before her date. Once in a while she'd drop me a crumb about someone she'd met online who was interested in her work. When she finally told me what was going on and that they were meeting up, I suggested he might be catfishing her. She laughed it off. I wish she hadn't."

"What's catfishing?" Helen asked, because it conjured up images of throwing a line into the river, not dating.

"It's when folks use social media to pretend to be someone they're not in order to lure unsuspecting people into relationships."

"It's a con game," Helen said simply.

"Yes."

Sarah went silent, and Helen wondered if she should say something, remind Sarah that none of this was her fault—whatever *this* was—but she knew it wouldn't do a bit of good. Instead she turned to look out the window again.

She took in the rise of the river, the tiny islands in its midst that looked to be drowning, the stalled barge traffic and chunks of debris visible above the ripple of the current. Then the thump of tires on the highway began to lull her, and she closed her eyes.

When next she opened them, an hour had passed, and they were rolling down an exit ramp in Belleville.

As Helen blinked the sleep from her eyes and got her bearings, Sarah guided the Jeep past a host of strips malls and gas stations before reaching an older residential area filled with generous lots, detached garages, and one-story ranches.

"We're almost there," Sarah told her.

Helen settled her hands over the purse in her lap, checking out the neighborhood: the plethora of pickup trucks, the roofs with pizza pie–sized satellite dishes, and the oversized dogs barking behind chain-link fences.

Sarah peered over the wheel, quietly counting the numbers painted on the mailboxes until she let out a soft "Aha. This must be it."

The Jeep stopped at the curb in front of a house that looked tidy enough: neat red brick, black shutters, and a small fenced-in front yard without much in the way of landscaping. A lengthy and very cracked asphalt driveway ran back toward a one-car garage, and a small sign on the gate of the fence very clearly stated: NO SOLICITORS. NO TRESPASSING.

Sarah popped out of the driver's side and came around to Helen's door then waited until she'd gotten out of the car. "You're coming with me, right?" the sheriff's wife asked, suddenly timid. "You're so good with people, talking to them and getting them to open up. I feel like I irritate people sometimes when I don't mean to."

*You don't say?*

"So you want me to take the lead?"

"Oh, would you?" Sarah smiled nervously. "Frank claims you have a Miss Marple complex. I just think you pay attention more than most."

Helen laughed. "I'll take that as a compliment."

She followed the sheriff's wife as she walked up the broken sidewalk and pushed open the gate, heading toward the covered front stoop. There was an iron railing and posts that had a trellis-like appearance, though the white paint had peeled and the concrete floor had split. Helen figured both were original to the 1950s-era house.

She wondered if Penny Tuttle was original to the house, as well.

Sarah cleared her throat as she rang the doorbell, stepping back to stand beside Helen as she waited for someone to answer.

When no one appeared within a minute or two, she gave Helen a look and pressed the bell again. "Maybe I should have called first," she said. "Although that would have just warned her off if she had something to do with Luann going missing."

Helen didn't bother to remind her that the rest of the town didn't think Luann was a missing woman so much as a besotted midlifer.

"Perhaps you could leave a note and ask her to call you," Helen suggested just as she saw movement beyond the storm door.

Sarah scuttled behind Helen, like a scared little girl.

The inner door opened, and a woman stood behind the glass, staring out at them, a most puzzled expression on her face. She had short iron-gray hair and speckled skin. Her button-front dress looked a bit speckled, too. Even the floral pattern couldn't mask the stains.

Helen thought she looked unwell.

"I'm guessing she's not a museum curator or appraiser," Sarah whispered over her shoulder. "She looks like my crazy aunt Thelma."

Helen shushed her.

The woman leaned near enough to the glass to fog it with her breath as she squinted, like she'd lost her specs. She fumbled about reaching for the door handle but seemed unable to get it open.

When Sarah didn't react, Helen went forward to help.

She drew the door wide quite easily, and the woman teetered then stumbled out onto the rubber welcome mat, still hanging on to the handle.

"Oh, dear," Helen said, trying to balance the storm door against her hip and steady the woman at the same time. When she was finally able to get the woman safely out and onto the porch, she let the storm door drop. "I'm sorry. I didn't mean to trip you up. You must be Penny Tuttle?"

"Who are you? Did Jackie send you?" the woman asked with the same bewildered look in her eyes. She rubbed her hands down over her hips.

"I'm sorry, I don't know Jackie. I'm Helen Evans from River Bend, and I've come looking for a friend named Luann Dupree. We thought you might have been in touch with her. She had written down your phone number, and she's been gone awhile, enough so that we're worried about her—"

"I don't know you," the woman said again.

"No, you don't," Helen agreed and found herself slowing down her speech and raising her voice, wondering if the woman was hard of hearing. "Do you know a woman named Luann Dupree? We're wondering if she's been in touch with you."

"Dupree . . . Dupree . . . I don't know Dupree, and I don't know you," the woman said, sounding panicked. She quickly turned away, grabbing at the door, letting out a string of curses and batting away Helen's hand when she offered assistance.

Finally, she made her way back inside. The glass in the storm door shuddered as it clunked closed, the heavier wood door shutting behind it.

Helen didn't know what else to do. She turned to Sarah, ready to say, "That's it! We're done. Can we go now?"

Only Sarah wasn't there.

*For Pete's sake!*

She'd promised not to sneak off, but she wasn't anywhere that Helen could see from the front stoop. The Jeep sat empty at the curb. Where the heck had she gone?

Helen hurried away from the door, looking this way and that. She spotted a neighbor across the chain-link fence: a heavyset woman with a hard look in her eye.

"Hey, what are you doing over there?" she called to Helen. "You're not Penny's regular nurse. What's going on?"

"We're just leaving," she called back, hoping to reassure the woman.

But the neighbor put a phone up to her ear, like she was calling the cops, and Helen didn't want to stick around to find out if that was what she was doing.

*Dang it, Sarah,* she thought. *Where are you?*

Helen crossed the grass toward the driveway, hurrying around the corner so fast she nearly tripped over a downspout. She spotted Sarah lurking around the garage, peering through the dusty windows.

"Hey!" she called out, because Sarah had gone around toward the side door. "We've got to go," she was saying, watching as Sarah picked up a rock from an overgrown plant bed and raised it, like she was going to break the glass panes. "Stop it!"

Her voice made the sheriff's wife hesitate, and Helen approached her, breathing hard.

"Put that down!" she demanded.

Reluctantly, Sarah lowered her arm.

"Good God," she muttered and straightened cockeyed glasses as she looked into Sarah's flushed face. "What the heck are you doing? I told you, no poking around, and definitely no breaking and entering! Do you want the sheriff to have to bail us out of the St. Clair County lockup?"

Sarah sighed and dropped the rock. "Let's go," she said as she started walking toward the Jeep. Helen shook her head and followed.

The woman from across the fence came out of her yard, the phone in her hand. "I'm glad I keep an eye on things next door! Jackie says no one should be here. The nurse came already today. You're trespassing!" she yelled as Sarah scrambled into the driver's seat while Helen got into the passenger's side.

Helen was shaking as she belted herself in, and Sarah turned the engine on and jerked the car away from the curb.

"Just what do you think you were doing?" Helen sputtered, bracing a hand on the dash as Sarah drove through the subdivision faster than the posted speed limit.

"I was looking for clues," she said, her cheeks a bright red.

"You were about to break the glass on the door!"

"I saw something in the garage, but I couldn't get in," Sarah protested. "What else was I supposed to do?"

"Not that!" Helen said and thanked her lucky stars she'd stopped her in time. "Just what did you see that warranted burglary?"

"Evidence," the sheriff's wife said, and her eyes took on an odd sparkle.

"You found evidence that Luann was there," Helen repeated, finding it impossible to hide her sarcasm.

"Yes, as a matter of fact, I did"—Sarah glanced at her sideways—"if you think finding Lu's car counts."

## Chapter 19

"It's HER CAR, I know it," Sarah insisted as they headed back to River Bend. "I'm sure it was a Fiat Spider, though it had a sheet draped across it."

"If it had a sheet over it, how could you tell?" Helen asked point-blank.

"Well, it was a small car, and it was bright red, just like Lu's Fiat." After thinking for a minute, she added, "The rims on her tires were gunmetal, something Lu specially ordered, and there was that little circle of red in the center. They're hard to miss."

"Could you see the license plate?" That at least would give the sheriff something concrete to go on.

Sarah's face fell. "No, the corner of the sheet covered the rear plate. But I caught part of a bumper sticker. Lu has a shovel-shaped one that says 'I dig history,' which is yellow. I could see the part that looks like a handle."

Helen kind of doubted that a description of a small red car with gunmetal rims and a hint of a yellow bumper sticker was enough for the sheriff to get a warrant to search the garage or the house.

"Anything else?"

"Just a gut feeling." Sarah was quiet for a minute. "Why would she have written down Penny Tuttle's phone number and stuck it in her book? I was meant to find it. We were meant to come here."

"Maybe Mrs. Tuttle has her own Fiat Spider. Luann isn't the only person in Illinois who owns one. For all we know, they could have even been in a car club together, which would be why Luann had her phone number."

Sarah let her gaze drift from the highway ahead long enough to give Helen a sideways glance. "Lu wasn't in a car club, and I highly doubt that the confused old woman who came to the door drives a Spider."

"Point taken," Helen said before she offered another theory. "If that was Luann's car—and I'm not saying it is—maybe she sold it before taking off so she'd have more money to travel."

"Absolutely not! Lu wouldn't have sold the Fiat for anything. It was her baby. She bought it for herself back when she turned fifty. She told me I'd have to pry her bony fingers from the steering wheel when she passed away."

"Sometimes people say things they mean at the time, only times change. Perhaps getting into an online relationship made Luann rethink her life," Helen replied, knowing nothing she could say would convince Sarah she was making a mistake.

Although it seemed Sarah had already moved on to another line of thought.

"If her car's in Belleville, she's still in the area. I'm sure of it. I just have to figure out where he's got her. Do you think she's a prisoner in Penny Tuttle's basement chained to a plumbing stack?" Sarah asked and her foot got a little heavy on the gas as they sped back to River Bend.

"You think she's chained in that old woman's basement?"

*Dear Lord.*

Helen leaned back into the headrest, deciding it was futile to argue.

The "find" had only seemed to fuel Sarah's belief that Luann had been taken and, now, that Penny Tuttle—or someone close to her—had something to do with it.

Helen couldn't imagine that Mrs. Tuttle had kidnapped anyone.

The woman appeared too frail and out of sorts. Something about that fragile appearance had reminded Helen of Bernie Winston.

As Sarah rattled on, trying to piece together a scenario about Luann's disappearance that suddenly involved Mrs. Tuttle in Belleville, Helen turned toward the window, staring out at the scenery and listening to the thump of the tires on the River Road.

The noise lulled her, and despite herself, she fell

asleep again. She was shaken awake by the Jeep pulling off the highway into tiny Elsah.

Sarah kept silent as they wound through the quaint village and ended up on the back road that would take them to River Bend.

It wasn't until they'd pulled in front of Helen's house and Sarah put the car in Park that she resumed her wild deductions.

"The next-door neighbor mentioned someone named Jackie. Maybe it's this Jackie who took Luann."

Helen unbuckled her belt, though her stiff fingers slowed her progress. "We don't even know if Jackie is male or female."

"It sounds like a nickname."

"You could try talking to Mrs. Tuttle or her neighbor, instead of picking up rocks to use as sledgehammers."

"Right!" Sarah hit a hand on the steering wheel. "We have to figure out how the Tuttles are involved in all this."

Helen hoped that "we" meant Sarah and the sheriff. She wanted nothing further to do with Sarah's snooping. She had begun to agree with the townsfolk who thought Sarah was grasping at straws and trying to make excuses for the friend who'd dumped her instead of moving on with her life without Luann.

"If I tell Frank about the car, I'm sure he'll want to help," Sarah said as Helen reached for the door and let herself out. "Maybe he'll finally file an official missing-person report on Luann and start investigating."

"Good luck," Helen said, uttering a terse good-bye before slamming the door.

She picked her way through the shallow floodwaters, sighing with relief when she reached the porch. As she leaned over to remove her boots, she heard the Jeep slosh through the muck as it pulled away. Once her boots were off, she locked the screen door to deter any more drop-in visitors.

"I'm home!" she trilled as she tugged wide the French doors to the interior.

Amber bounded out full throttle, voicing his displeasure at being cooped inside for so long. He sprang atop a table that had once been a crank washing machine. (Helen had bought it at Agnes's shop long ago.) Though he couldn't go beyond the porch, at least from there he could watch the birds flit about and see the creek water spilling into the street, along with the occasional swimming snake that made Helen shudder.

While Amber surveyed the outdoors, Helen made a beeline for the kitchen. She turned the oven to 350 degrees and set about making a tuna casserole. Then she sat down at the dining room table with the crossword from the morning's paper, which she still hadn't finished. By the time the oven timer dinged, she had filled in the last squares.

"Nine-letter word for 'dirty dog,'" she read and easily filled in the missing pieces to form *scoundrel*.

With that, she set down her purple pen and the folded newsprint, and she dashed into the kitchen to rescue the casserole from the oven. She made herself a pimento-cheese sandwich for dinner, not expecting to be invited to stay when she dropped off the tuna dish with Betty Winston.

She made sure Amber had dinner before she left. Considering it was sardines in shrimp jelly and smelled like the harbor when the water was low, Helen was eager to take off for a while. Cradling the warm casserole in its sleeve, she used her free hand to set the hook lock on the screen door so her fur-child couldn't paw his way out in her absence. Then she sloshed across Jersey Avenue and crossed to Springfield, trying hard to ignore the moving current of floodwaters in the creek that gurgled onto the bridge beneath her green frog galoshes.

A few friendly souls called out hellos from front porches as she passed. Otherwise, things were their usual calm. There was no crowd gathered in front of Betty and Bernie's as there had been earlier in the day. In fact, it was so quiet she could hear the rush of the floodwater beyond the homes on the right-hand side of the street.

The engine gunned in a pickup truck that had been parked across the way, and the vehicle slid past her as she turned onto Bernie and Betty's front walk.

She'd barely raised a fist to knock when the door swung wide from within. At the sight of Helen standing on the welcome mat, Clara's face broke into a relieved smile.

"It's tuna casserole," she said, handing over her offering.

"Thank goodness it's you," her friend said, quickly ushering her in. "I do appreciate how concerned the town is about Bernie, but even though the sheriff spread the word to leave us in peace, it's been one visitor after another. I've been turning them all away, though they keep leaving things, of course."

"Things" being the baskets and Tupperware containers holding muffins and cookies, enough to feed an army. Helen spotted the load on the buffet in the dining room as they walked through to the kitchen.

She wondered where Bernie was, as she didn't see either him or Betty. She did catch the white noise of a TV on in the back den, and she heard a child's voice. Sawyer, she assumed.

Clara turned on the oven to Warm. She didn't speak until she had the casserole out of its sleeve and had slipped it in. "We'll have this for dinner," she said. "Thank you."

"You're welcome."

Her friend motioned her toward the breakfast table, and Helen settled into a chair. "Would you like coffee? I'd just poured myself a fresh cup when you knocked."

"No, I'm good."

Clara grabbed a cup from the counter and brought it to the table with her. "Ellen's staying overnight," she said as she sat down. "Having her and Sawyer around definitely helps lift the mood."

"How is Bernie?"

"He's as crazy as a loon, but he's fine otherwise. I

think he's going to outlive me and Betty both," Clara muttered before blowing on her brew. She started to take a sip but set it down with a sigh. "I do believe it's time for Betty to take a different tack. This can't go on, or she'll lose her mind, as well."

"How is Betty?"

"She's a basket case. She's popping antianxiety medication like candy so she doesn't fall apart."

Clara paused to blot her eyes with a napkin.

"I'm sorry," Helen said, for all the good it did.

"I know you are, and I'm so grateful that—" Clara stopped midsentence as Betty appeared in the archway.

If Clara's older sister was surprised to see Helen, she didn't show it. Her eyes were on Clara alone.

"Sissy," she said. Her voice sounded dull. "Could you help me with Bernie? He won't let me change him, and he's soaking wet."

"Yes, of course." Clara instantly rose, pushing back her chair, and headed toward the doorway as Betty disappeared.

Before she got out of the kitchen, Ellen popped in from the den. "I heard Mom," she said. "Is there anything I can do?"

"No," Clara told her, waving a hand. "You sit and keep Helen company for a few minutes until I'm back."

"Sure."

Helen smiled half-heartedly as Ellen came around the table and sat down. The younger woman pushed mud-brown hair behind her ears. She had soft creases at her eyes and mouth, but her skin seemed unlined otherwise. *Good genes,* Helen thought. Both Clara and Betty had looked youthful well into their early sixties.

"Sawyer's watching *The Lego Movie* for the hundredth time," Ellen remarked, and her gaze shifted toward the den. A high-pitched laugh tickled the air, and Betty and Bernie's daughter smiled fleetingly. "She's a good kid."

"Does she understand what's going on with her grandfather?"

"I think she does. She knows he's got a disease called Alzheimer's that affects his brain. She gets that he can't remember who we are most of the time. She likes to say that Grandpa has faulty wiring."

Helen nodded. "That's a smart thing for a young girl to realize."

Ellen put her elbows on the table and set her chin in her hands. "She's more accepting than I am. I'm not finding it as easy as I thought to just roll with whatever happens. Strangely enough, at first it was kind of fun, like playacting, going along with whatever he said. We were traveling to coal mines or at a cocktail party, or some random person at the grocery store was the president of the company and we had to go chat with him."

"It's got to be hard."

"Yes," Ellen said, and tears came to her eyes. "It's been especially difficult lately. He's been saying things that are so hurtful. Oh, I know, it's not really him. It's the disease talking, right?"

"Yes."

"But that doesn't make it any easier when he tells Mom that he wants to ask the grocery store checkout girl to marry him, or talks to her like he thinks *she's* his mother. And he can't seem to remember at all that I'm his daughter."

"That's normal," Helen said quietly.

Ellen wiped at her tears as they slipped down her cheeks. "It's normal not to remember people, yes. But he seems to have forgotten entirely that he had a child. He insists I'm not his."

Helen touched her arm. "You can't hold it against him. He's not the same person anymore. This Bernie Winston . . . his life is made up of scrambled pieces, fragments of who he used to be. You can't fault him for losing his past. Sawyer's right. He has faulty wiring. Things just don't connect."

"I get what you're saying," Ellen told her. "My mom and aunt have said the same things when they've heard my dad tell me I don't exist. But it stings nonetheless."

Helen was patting Ellen's arm when Clara returned.

"Thank God that's done," she said, rubbing hands together. "Now maybe we can sit down to some dinner. Helen brought a tuna casserole."

"Great," Ellen said, giving Helen a wane smile as she got up. "Sawyer loves that. I'll go get her."

"You'll stay, Helen, won't you?" Clara asked as Ellen left the room.

"No, I've eaten already," she replied, rising from the

table. "I should go and leave you all alone. You've been through enough today. You don't need guests."

Clara didn't protest. Instead she nodded and headed toward the front door, though Helen hardly expected to be walked out.

"If you need me . . ."

"You'll be there," Clara finished for her. "I hope that offer's good forever."

"There's no expiration date," Helen assured her. She would have laughed under ordinary circumstances. But this wasn't that.

"Good night, dear friend."

"Good night," she said as Clara slowly shut the door.

## *Chapter 20*

---

IT WAS JUST after supper when Frank finally gave in to Sarah's badgering. He didn't have it in him to argue, not with how he'd been working nonstop with the flood lapping at the storefronts on Main Street, dealing with panicked homeowners and the Department of Transportation shutting down the stretch of highway into River Bend, not to mention chasing down a lost citizen.

"Hop in the car," he told her, setting his napkin on the table. "Forget dessert. We'll go into Belleville if that's what you want."

"We will?"

What Frank wanted to say was: *If that's what'll get you to pipe down about Luann Dupree, then, yes, we'll go right now.* But he bit his cheek and replied instead, very simply, "Yes, dear."

He hadn't been able to enjoy his fried chicken and

mashed potatoes with her ranting about finding Luann Dupree's car in an elderly woman's garage and insisting he dig deeper.

"She's my friend, Frank, and she's been missing for weeks! It's high time you did something!"

"What the heck were you doing, poking around a total stranger's property?" he asked, and he felt a familiar twinge in his belly. If it was an ulcer eating a hole in his stomach, well, he'd earned it.

"I took Helen Evans with me," his wife said, giving him an innocent look, as if having a chaperone absolved her of wrongdoing.

"But you lied to me and said you were visiting a friend. Why'd you go at all?"

"Luann pointed me in that direction," Sarah told him. "I just had to be patient and listen."

"Listen?" he repeated. "So you've talked to her, have you?"

"Not exactly." Sarah had glanced down at her plate, where she'd been pushing around mashed potatoes and green beans, building a wall around a poor drumstick that that she'd been too busy to eat. The way she avoided his eyes meant either the truth was being stretched or she was embarrassed.

"Luann e-mailed you?"

"No."

"You got a text?" Frank tried next, only to earn a shake of his wife's mop of hair.

"I found a note she'd written a while back stuck in

her favorite book about pirates," Sarah said, starting slowly and then building steam. "So I went online, got the address, and drove over there with Helen. While she tried to talk to the homeowner, who was completely off her rocker, I kind of wandered around and saw a car in the garage that looked exactly like Luann's."

*Kind of wandered?*

When Frank shook his head, Sarah snapped at him, "You can't let this go, I won't let you!" She had a tight look on her face that he knew meant trouble, unless he desired to sleep on the couch. "My friend needs my help, and I need yours."

He'd about had it with Luann Dupree. Her belongings took up nearly the whole of their one-car garage. And now his wife was playing detective and bothering strangers in an effort to "help" a woman who, as far as Frank was aware, was right where she wanted to be. Weren't her e-mails to the city council resigning her job and professing to be on a great adventure proof enough of that?

"Let's get this over with," he grumbled. *"Now."*

Then Frank did something he rarely ever did except in dire emergencies: he left the table with his meal unfinished. He herded his wife into his cruiser and put the Belleville address of Penny Tuttle into his GPS, and they headed out.

It wasn't yet dark, but the sky had begun to mellow. The bright blue of afternoon had evolved into a cloudy smear of purplish pink.

As he drove, his wife talked. That was just how it went. She repeated things she'd told him countless times already: about Luann's mysterious online relationship that culminated in a date with Mr. Maybe the night before she vanished, the ensuing e-mails that were bland to the point of uselessness, the absence of phone calls or selfies, and the abandoned accounts on social media.

Frank had heard it all before a million times. So if it took going to Belleville to get Sarah to let go, it was worth it.

When they finally got off the highway and made their way to the subdivision of the woman named Penny Tuttle, the streetlights had come on, the light they shed dim.

Sarah pointed out the house as soon as they turned a corner.

Frank stopped the car right in front, cut the engine, and turned to his wife.

She had already taken off her seat belt and was reaching for the door when he put his hand on her arm.

"Ground rules," he said, because he knew they would need them.

He heard the irritated whoosh of her breath as she faced him.

"You let me take the lead," he began, "and I do the talking. You stay right by my side, and most importantly, you don't wander."

"You sound just like her, you know," Sarah told him.

"Who?"

"Helen Evans."

Frank's cheeks warmed, and he grunted.

Mrs. Evans could be a thorn in his side at times, but he had to admire her for trying to keep Sarah out of trouble.

"Okay, let's go."

Sarah sat and waited for him to come around to her side of the car. He opened the door, helped her out, and held on to her arm even after.

"Can't we look in the garage first?" she asked, trying to tug away.

"No."

The porch light flicked on as they approached, so Frank knew they'd been seen. Although these days folks were as apt to keep the lights off and *not* open the door when they spotted a cruiser parked in front of their home.

A woman came to stand behind the storm door. She scowled as they came up the porch steps from the sidewalk.

"That's the nosy neighbor," Sarah hissed under her breath. "She threatened to call the police on Helen and me."

*With good reason,* Frank thought.

He shushed his wife, though he let go, clearing his throat as they reached the other side of the welcome mat.

The woman emerged, letting the storm door slap shut. She stood with her arms crossed, clearly guarded.

"Good evening, ma'am," Frank said and tipped his hat. "I'm Sheriff Biddle . . ."

"Did you bring this woman for me to identify?" she interrupted, jerking her chin at Sarah. "She was trespassing earlier. Did Jackie call the cops and report it? I told him everything."

"Jackie?" Frank repeated.

"Mrs. Tuttle's son. It's her house, although she's not well. She's inside resting." The woman frowned. "I'm Ezra Bick from next door. I keep an eye on the place while Jackie's away."

"I apologize for my wife," Frank said. Though Sarah snorted, she did not speak. "But she's very concerned about a friend of hers named Luann Dupree and thought she might be here . . ."

"There's no Luann Dupree in this house," Mrs. Bick cut him off again, and her eyes narrowed. "There's only Penny now, and the home health-care people that Jackie hired, who come and go. Penny's not well. She's got dementia and diabetes and nerve issues, you name it." The woman twirled a hand in the air. "I tried to help, but dealing with all her meds got too confusing."

"I know Luann was here!" Sarah piped up and pointed toward the driveway that ran alongside the house. "I saw her car in the garage! It's a red Fiat Spider with gunmetal-gray rims. I know it was here. So where is she?"

"May we look in the garage?" Frank asked the neighbor, because it was the one thing that was going to settle this. "We'd appreciate having the owner's permission, of course."

"Since you're so polite, Sheriff, I'll see about that." The woman glared at Sarah as she answered. "Give me a minute, and I'll call Jackie. He makes all the decisions for Penny these days."

Mrs. Bick plucked a phone from her pants pocket and went back inside. Frank could see her through the storm door. He watched her press the touch pad and put the phone to her ear. She wandered away as she spoke, though Frank could hear mumbles. Then she returned to the door, the phone still at her ear. She nodded before putting it away.

She came back out. "Jackie says I can take you to the garage. So come on."

With that, she took off, striding down from the porch and marching around the corner of the house. Sarah hurried after her.

Frank hiked up his pants and followed.

"Stay here," Mrs. Bick told them when they reached the façade with its faux-paneled aluminum door. She took some keys from her pocket and stabbed one into the side garage door. She disappeared for an instant before a rumble rent the air.

Slowly, the metal door rattled open.

Sarah let out a strangled cry, and Frank quickly realized why.

The garage was empty.

The car was gone.

## Chapter 21

*Wednesday*

HELEN HAD STAYED up for the late news, waiting for the weatherman to report on whether or not the river had reached its crest. When he'd finally shown the graphics illustrating the fact that they'd already hit peak flood stage at Grafton—the nearest neighbor River Bend had that rated a spot on the map—Helen had let out a whoop that startled Amber off the bed.

"We're almost out of the woods! Pretty soon you'll be able to chase mice again," she'd told the departing cat as she watched his tail end disappear out the door.

After a deep shoulder-raising breath, she'd shut down the TV and reached over to switch off the bedside light. Then she'd plumped up her pillow and settled beneath the covers with a smile.

Her final thoughts before she'd nodded off were pleasant ones. Bernie Winston was safe. The spring flood was almost over. The Mighty Mississippi would soon begin to retreat. Within a week or two the creeks would shrink back within their banks, the streets would dry up, and the harbor residents who'd had to leave their homes could return. The pool would need a good scrubbing, and the softball field would remain mushy for a month. But it was enough to know they were about to turn the corner.

It would not be another Great Flood of '93.

Thank God for that.

Weary to the bone, Helen didn't wake up once until the sun cut a yellow line around the window drapes in her bedroom.

She blinked drowsily and gave a good stretch before kicking back the covers and taking care of her morning routine.

She had high hopes for the day, even if she couldn't put on her sneakers to take her usual walk to the river and back.

Humming, she turned on the coffeepot then grabbed a new can of Fancy Feast for Amber. The cat heard the snap of her popping off the lid and trotted into the kitchen lickety-split. While he feasted on ocean whitefish, she refilled his water bowl before grabbing a bagel from the fridge to toast.

She would sit on the porch with her breakfast this morning and do her crossword without interruption. Didn't she deserve that after yesterday's insanity?

By the time she'd gotten a mug filled with coffee and

slapped a little butter on her bagel, Amber had already settled on the porch table. He sat smack atop the newspaper, one hind leg raised as he preened.

Yeesh.

The best-laid plans and all that.

Helen didn't have the heart to shove him off, so she settled on the wicker sofa, deciding just to take in the scene beyond the porch screen for entertainment. She'd do the crossword later, after Amber finished giving himself a bath.

More buds on tree limbs had opened, and the emerging green leaves had thickened, blotting out bits of the blue sky above. Birds twittered back and forth, as if sharing a tasty bit of gossip. Even the rush of the swollen creek couldn't dim her good mood. She'd almost gotten used to seeing the water on the road. It gave her the perfect excuse to put on those frog boots from her granddaughter again.

Too much excitement the day before had left her craving a nice boring morning. If only Amber would get off the newsprint, she could start on that crossword . . .

*Whoop whoop whoop.*

The bleat of a siren broke apart the quiet of the morning. The noise nearly made Helen's heart stop.

"What the heck," she murmured, waiting to hear the sound again, but it didn't come.

Then she saw the sheriff's black-and-white approaching from the direction of Main Street. Instantly, she was up on her feet.

The water in the street slowed the vehicle's progress, but still it plowed through the brown slop, leaving ripples in its wake.

For some reason, she expected the car to turn toward the bridge onto Springfield, but instead it stopped right in front of her house. The vehicle shimmied as the sheriff got out and made his way forward in knee-high rubber boots.

*Oh, no,* Helen thought, afraid to move. Was the sheriff here for *her?* Had Sarah told them about their excursion into Belleville? Or worse, had that neighbor of Penny Tuttle's gotten Sarah's plate number and reported them for trespassing?

She left her bagel half-eaten and her coffee half-drunk and hurried over to the door as Frank Biddle clomped up her steps. He raised a fist to knock but paused when he saw Helen standing there in front of him.

"I'm sorry about the siren, ma'am. I hit it by mistake," the sheriff apologized. "It's been one of those mornings."

"Am I in trouble?" Helen asked instinctively.

"You?" He scrunched up his brow. "No, it's just that there's been a . . . Um, well, I have some bad news." He stumbled over his words before he cleared his throat. "Look, I am sorry to bother you so early, but will you come with me, please?"

Go with him?

Helen thought that sounded an awful lot like an echo of Sarah Biddle's plea yesterday to go sleuthing.

Why had she let that woman talk her into it? Next time, whatever Sarah asked, she'd tell her no. She wasn't sure if she could do that to the sheriff, however.

"This doesn't have to do with Luann Dupree, does it?" she asked, half-afraid he was going to slap her in handcuffs. "I don't know what your wife told you, but I had no part in snooping around that woman's garage . . ."

"It's Bernie Winston, ma'am." He stopped her protest, hardly looking angry. In fact, quite the opposite. His bulldog's face appeared unshaven, and his eyes had gray circles beneath. Certainly, dealing with the flood had taken its toll on him, as had the search for Bernie yesterday. But there was something more in his eyes, something very somber. "Could you come with me to the house, please? I think the family will appreciate having you there when I fill them in on his whereabouts."

"So he's taken off again?" Helen asked.

Had Bernie gotten himself hurt? she wondered. Was he in the hospital? Did the sheriff imagine Helen's presence would soften the blow when he updated the family?

"Mr. Winston got out again, yes, sometime in the night, apparently. Mrs. Winston woke up this morning, and he was gone. But he's been found."

Helen put a hand to her heart. "Well, that's a relief."

The sheriff didn't look relieved. In fact, if anything, he looked more morose than before. "I got a call from Larry Overstreet at the end of Springfield not five minutes ago. He said the floodwaters brought something banging against his porch supports in back where the creek had risen so high."

"And he saw Bernie?" Helen offered.

"You could say that, yes, ma'am," Frank Biddle told her and cleared his throat. He tugged at the knot of his tie, and Helen realized he was trying to compose himself. "He was caught in the current of the creek, Mrs. Evans. Larry fished him out, but he wasn't breathing."

Bernie's body was the thing banging against the Overstreets' back porch?

*Dear Lord.*

"Was he given CPR? Was he all right?"

"No, ma'am, he's not all right."

Helen's chest tightened. "You can't mean that he's . . . You're not saying that he's—" She couldn't finish.

"Yes, ma'am, he is, and I am," the sheriff replied. "Bernie Winston is dead."

## Chapter 22

BETTY WINSTON INSISTED on seeing her husband.

It wasn't that she didn't believe the sheriff or even Doc Melville, who'd taken custody of the body, explaining that he needed to give Bernie a careful once-over before he declared cause of death and released him to the funeral parlor.

Amos Melville was thorough. She would give him that.

But what Betty sorely needed was to look at her husband with her own two eyes, or she couldn't accept that he was dead.

As the sheriff stood awkwardly in the living room, twisting his hat in his hands, Helen Evans sat beside her, saying how sorry she was and offering to help in any way she could. Betty felt like she was trapped a nightmare, one that had lasted for far, far too long. She wished someone would shake her hard to wake her up so that this whole horrible ordeal would be over, just another of those bad dreams her sleeping pills sometimes caused.

She saw Ellen crying and hugging Sawyer, Clara watching them from nearby with tears in her eyes.

Oddly enough, Betty's own eyes were dry. She had already cried so much.

"This shouldn't have happened, you know. There should be a cure by now for this. No one should have to suffer the way we've suffered," she had stopped the sheriff midcondolences to say. "I want *my* Bernie back."

"I'm sorry, ma'am."

*Sorry.* She had heard that so often it barely registered anymore.

What if the sheriff was wrong and Bernie would return, like he had the day before? Nothing would change and their lives would go on. He would be as loopy as ever. He still wouldn't know if she was his wife or his mother or a stranger. He would clomp around the house in his boxer shorts and golf cleats or rearrange the furniture in the den for the hundredth time. He would awaken her in the middle of the night, shrieking about a deer running up the hallway or a car trying to run him down, and she would do her best to calm him down and reassure him that everything was all right. She would keep his bedclothes clean and dry, no matter how often they had to be changed. She would keep Bernie clean and dry, no matter how often she had to change *him.*

And she would feed him, bathe him, and finish his sentences. She would listen to his disjointed ramblings and pretend they were conversations. She would try to remember him as he once was: the man she'd fallen in love with, the man who'd worked so hard to provide for the family that Betty had always wanted. The partner who had held her hand when she'd miscarried so many times and who had played nursemaid during her bout with breast cancer.

Betty shook her head, finding it all too much to bear.

"Would you like to see him?" the sheriff asked. "Sometimes it helps people, makes it real. Other times it makes it worse."

*How much worse could it get?*

She lifted her gaze to meet Frank Biddle's. "Yes, I want to see him," she said, "right now, please."

"Uh, sure, ma'am, let me just call Doc," he told her and went out to the porch to get on his phone.

Betty told Clara to stay with Ellen and Sawyer while the sheriff drove her to Doc's office, a trip that took all of two minutes, just enough time for Betty to go over what she'd been told about her husband.

Bernie had been found in the flooded creek a couple of houses away.

He had been pulled from the water not breathing. He'd had no pulse. Despite attempts at CPR, his heart could not be made to beat again. Doc Melville had been called to the scene and had pronounced death.

Amos Melville patted her hand when they arrived at

his office. "Hello, Mrs. Winston, I'm so sorry for your loss."

*Sorry.*

There was that word again.

"Where is he?" Betty asked, wondering if Bernie was lying in an exam room or if Doc had some kind of morgue with a big ol' refrigerator like the funeral home and the county hospital.

"Are you sure you want to do this?" Doc Melville asked rather than answering her question. He peered at her through his bifocals, his bushy brows knitted.

Betty swallowed. "Yes."

She was glad for the medication she'd taken, thankful for the calm it made her feel when otherwise she would have been a nervous wreck. Still, her hands shook as Doc preceded her into the back room and gently pulled away the white sheet he'd draped over Bernie's body. He folded it at the shoulders. Then Doc stepped away.

Despite herself, Betty let out a small cry when she saw Bernie's face. There were scratches and mottled bruises on his brow and cheeks. His eye sockets seemed sunken and gray.

"Oh, God, how did it ever come to this?" she whispered, going nearer. She reached out a trembling hand to touch him. He felt cold, waxy. His eyes were closed, thankfully, as she didn't think she could bear to look into them. "You are in a better place now, aren't you?" she asked, though his colorless lips did not move in response. "You're whole again, I'm sure of it. You're *you*. When I see you again, you will be the man I fell in love with. You will wait for me . . . remember me . . . won't you?"

When she turned to tell Doc she was done, he looked at her with moist eyes. He lifted his specs from his nose to wipe at them. Then he gently drew the sheet over Bernie's head like a shroud.

"Come," he said gently.

Betty felt his hand at her elbow as he led her from the exam room and out to the waiting room, where Sheriff Biddle sat, his hat in his hands. Beside him was Helen Evans, who had tagged along at the sheriff's insistence even though Betty had told them it wasn't necessary. She wasn't going to fall apart. It was much too late for that.

"What can I do for you, ma'am?" Frank Biddle asked, quickly rising to his feet, though he kept his hat off, spinning it like a record player. "How might I help, other than take you home, I mean?"

"I need to make arrangements," Betty said, the monotone of her voice reflecting how dead she felt deep inside. "Bernie left a directive. He wanted to be cremated."

"Right."

"This stupid disease has taken such a toll on our lives. It's robbed us of years that we should have had. It made us different people and not always for the good—" Betty stopped to draw in a breath. "I don't want to drag it out further. I'm so tired, Sheriff. I'm so very, very tired."

"I'm sure you are." Biddle glanced over at Doc Melville. "Once there's a signed death certificate, you can do whatever needs doing."

"Will that take long?" she asked.

"Only as long as it takes me to confirm the cause of death," Doc said.

"But we know how he died." Betty sighed, impatient, wanting it all to be over with. "He slipped out of the house in the middle of the night, got lost, and fell into the creek. He must have drowned. Isn't it obvious?"

Doc patted her shoulder. "That would seem to be the general order of things, yes. Look, I promise to take good care of Mr. Winston, just like I've cared for most of the folks in this town, from birth onward. So there's no need to worry."

"I'll try," Betty said, though it wasn't exactly the truth. For years she had worried day and night. She didn't know how to do anything else.

"Hang it all. I almost forgot something," Doc said and disappeared back up the hallway for a bit before returning with a zippered baggie. "Your husband's wedding band is still on his finger. I can remove the ring if you'd like to have it . . ."

"No, no," Betty said, her stomach churning. "Please, leave it on."

"Then this is all I have to give you of his personal effects," he told her, holding out the baggie as Betty looked blankly at it.

Reluctantly, she took it, eyeing the contents through

the clear plastic: a thick black pen with lots of gold details. If she squinted through her glasses, she could make out CARTIER imprinted on a band on the pen's cap. "That can't be Bernie's," she said, trying to hand back the baggie to Doc. "He never owned a pen so fancy."

"But it was in the pocket of his pajama pants," Doc said, reluctantly taking the bag back. "Maybe he picked it up from somewhere and hung on to it."

"I guess he could have," Betty replied. "He's done so many strange things." Then she hesitated, blinking. "Hold on. I do recognize it." She turned to the sheriff, her voice angry as she told him, "It belongs to that awful man, Jackson Lee. I caught him at our house a while back, trying to bamboozle Bernie. He must have been conning Bernie out of our money for years. I've found canceled checks . . . contracts for oil wells and windmills and God knows what else that drained our bank account." She caught herself, took a deep breath. "Bernie didn't know what he was doing. Mr. Lee must have left that pen at our house when I chased him out. I saw it in Bernie's hand . . ."

"You should have called me, ma'am," Biddle said.

"There are a lot of things I should have done, Sheriff," she replied, thinking hard. She tapped a finger in the air. "I do believe I've seen his car since, parked across the street at odd hours. It's an older Cadillac. Black. It may have been there last night, too."

The sheriff plunked his hat on his head. "Jackson

Lee's car?" he repeated and took a few steps forward to get the bag from Doc. "You're sure?"

"Pretty sure."

"Jackson?" Helen Evans said, and her eyes widened as they looked at the sheriff. "Who is he?"

"Someone I need to talk to," the sheriff answered, pocketing the baggie.

"He's a liar and a thief," Betty spat. "If he had anything to do with Bernie . . . with what happened to Bernie, I want to know. He belongs behind bars as it is, targeting people like Bernie who don't have a wit about them." She started to shake, her whole body shuddering, and she couldn't seem to stop.

"Are you okay, ma'am?" Biddle said. "Doc, maybe she needs something?"

Betty turned to Doc Melville. "Just get this over with." Despite everything, she began to sob. "It needs to be over. It needs to be done."

The doctor reached out to steady her. "Mrs. Winston, perhaps I should give you a sedative . . ."

"I want to see Ellen and Sawyer," she howled and jerked away from Amos, addressing the sheriff again. "I need to get home. I need my family!"

"Yes, ma'am, we'll be on our way pronto." Frank Biddle went to the door to hold it wide for her.

"Let me help you—" Helen Evans approached to take her arm, but Betty somehow found the strength to shake off Helen's hand.

"I'll be fine," she insisted, sounding crosser than she meant to. "I just need time alone with my girls."

"Of course." Helen nodded.

Betty knew that if she'd been alone in the world, she would have thrown herself into the floodwaters after Bernie. But she couldn't. She had a daughter and a granddaughter to live for, and that was precisely what she planned to do.

## Chapter 23

"HELEN! OH, HELEN, wait up!"

Sarah Biddle chased her down as she left Doc Melville's place, not ten minutes after the sheriff had departed in the cruiser, driving Betty Winston home. Helen had stayed for a brief chat with Amos, the commiserating kind that one had after a contemporary passed away. They'd spoken of life being too short, of never knowing which day might be the last, of trying to escape the ills that seemed to plague so many in their sunset years. Helen asked, too, if Doc thought there was anything remotely suspicious about how Bernie had died, and he'd told her pretty much what he'd told Bernie's wife: "I won't release him to the mortuary until I've examined him. Soon as you go, I'll get started."

She had hardly gotten to the sidewalk when Sarah

hopped out of the door of her Jeep, looking bright eyed and bushy tailed and up to no good.

"Aha! Thank goodness I found you," she said, catching her breath. "I texted Frank and he said you'd stayed behind at Doc's. I heard about Bernie Winston. It's just awful, him falling into the creek. I'm so sorry."

"I am, too," Helen said solemnly. "But you might want to go pay your condolences to Betty Winston, not me."

"Oh, sure, I'll do that later." Sarah bobbed on her heels, not looking solemn in the least. "I don't know if Frank told you, but he went back to Belleville with me last night. He got the neighbor to let us into the garage—"

"Look, dear, I'm on my way home," Helen said, cutting her off. "It's been a trying morning, and I'm not in the mood to play Nancy Drew again. If the sheriff's going to help you snoop, that's wonderful. But I'm out. So if you'll excuse me, I've things to do."

She didn't care if she was being a bit rude. Sarah Biddle wasn't high on her list of favorite people at the moment.

Helen started to leave, but Sarah caught her hand.

"The red car was gone!" she said. "Don't you get what that means?"

"That someone drove it somewhere, as people tend to do with cars," Helen remarked, hoping that would be the end of it. But Sarah held on.

"It means we're onto something . . . that we're closing in on whoever has Luann. I think Penny Tuttle's son,

Jackie, is involved, and yes, it's a man. The neighbor said as much last night."

Helen thought suddenly of the name Jackson Lee. Was he the Jackie referred to by Penny Tuttle's neighbor? He was the con man that Betty Winston said took money from an irrational Bernie. Did he participate in other kinds of cons, too, perhaps the romantic kind? *Did* he have something to do with Luann's disappearance?

"So you found the mysterious Jackie?" Helen said, standing still.

"Well, not his location exactly, but I think he's near."

"He's in River Bend?"

"Could be." Sarah pursed her lips and glanced around them, as though the mysterious Jackie were lurking about, eavesdropping on them. "I might be able to flush him out," she said. "I just have to poke a hornet's nest."

Did Sarah know that the sheriff seemed intent on talking to the man named Jackson Lee, but in relation to Bernie's death, not Luann's disappearance?

"Maybe you should leave the poking to your husband."

"I knew you'd say that." Sarah sniffed. She dug into her right jacket pocket. "I found something else in Luann's belongings, and it might answer a lot of questions about why she was taken."

"Is it the mysterious artifact?" Helen asked, figuring it had to be small if it fit in Sarah's pocket.

"Um, no, not the artifact exactly, but I did find a clue, a real one," she added when Helen sighed.

Sarah retrieved a square of folded paper, larger than the one bearing the address in Belleville. Still, it made Helen wonder if Sarah wasn't just making these things up herself, so convinced that her friend was kidnapped that illusion was reality.

This time it wasn't a scribbled page from a memo pad; it was a computer-generated printout, deeply creased at the folds.

"Was this stuck in the pirate book, as well?" she asked dryly.

Sarah ignored her sarcasm. "Take a closer look," she said and pushed the sheet into Helen's hands.

It appeared to be an article from the *New York Times* over a decade old.

Squinting through her specs, she read the headline: MUSEUM FINDS LEWIS AND CLARK ARTIFACT LOST FOR A CENTURY.

Helen stood on the sidewalk, eyes skimming the first couple of paragraphs. It referenced a bear-claw necklace that had been donated to the Peabody Museum at Harvard and had been misplaced sometime after being catalogued in 1899. Finding it was akin to stumbling upon "a Vermeer in the attic," according to a Native American–art curator, a line that Luann had highlighted in yellow marker. The piece had thirty-eight claws measuring approximately three inches each, once painted with a red pigment, and had likely been given to the explorers by a tribal chief.

Helen looked up. "You think the Peabody Museum's missing necklace somehow ended up in River Bend?"

"No, not *that* one," Sarah said. "It's in a permanent exhibit with a handful of other artifacts that can directly be traced to the expedition." Her eyes brightened. "But what if there's more than one? What if Luann stumbled upon a necklace that had some kind of proof about its provenance that no one realized existed. She must have had something because . . . look here!" Sarah pointed to a scribble in the margin that seemed to say *Drop off Sat AM.*

"You think she dropped off the necklace somewhere on the Saturday morning before her date?"

"It's a distinct possibility."

"But you don't know where?"

Sarah shook her head. "I've e-mailed local museums and talked to a history professor at Principia College, but no one will admit to hearing anything about a newfound artifact that can be traced back to Lewis and Clark."

"You've been busy," Helen said, having to give her credit.

"It's all I've been doing since Luann disappeared. Trying to figure out what was so valuable that someone would want to kidnap Lu."

Helen gave back the article, which Sarah carefully folded and put in her pocket.

"If you sorted through Luann's things from her apartment—and looked around the Historical Society and didn't find it—what makes you believe it's still around?"

"Because the person who has Luann's phone is still communicating," Sarah said. "I got a text this morning about how breathtaking Yosemite is with a photo attached."

"What if it's really from Luann?"

"On a hunch I searched Google Images' catalog of pictures from Yosemite, and I found the shot within a minute. Luann didn't take that picture, and neither did her fictional boyfriend, not unless he works for *National Geographic*."

Helen hadn't seen that coming. "Oh."

"I guess Lu's kidnapper decided he'd better send a photo, or I wouldn't stop pestering."

Helen stuck her hands in the pockets of her warm-up jacket. She suddenly felt cold. "Where do you plan to go from here?"

Sarah Biddle's face turned positively stony. "I've narrowed down potential Mr. Maybes to white middle-aged males that could fit the generic description given by the bartender at the Loading Dock, either bearded or clean shaven, and I've cross-referenced with any new men who've come to town recently, and only one fits the mold. He used to teach history at a middle school in Caseyville, which is a stone's throw from Belleville. He's single, and it's entirely plausible he'd romance Luann and get her out of the way so he could rob from this Historical Society without anyone being the wiser."

"Is his name Jackson Lee?" Helen asked point-blank.

Sarah looked confused. "No, who's that?"

Instead of answering her question, Helen posed another. "So you've found someone else named Jackie?"

"Jack is a nickname for John, isn't it?" Sarah asked.

Helen saw where she was headed, and she wasn't sure if Sarah was nutty as a fruitcake or brilliant.

"You think Jackie is . . ."

"John Danielson, the new Historical Society director," Sarah finished for her. "It fits, doesn't it? I mean, he meets Lu in some history chat room, gets to know her, and gets her talking about her work. She tells him things, enough for him to put together a very neat plan to get Lu out of the way so he can take over. Who's to stop him from stealing the bear-claw necklace, or any of the other artifacts?"

"That's assuming there is a bear-claw necklace."

"Yes."

Helen felt too tired to play these games. "So you peg our new director as the kidnapper? You figure he met Luann for a date night in Grafton then lured her to the house in Belleville, stashed her in the basement, and hid her car in the garage? Do you even know if he's related to Penny Tuttle?"

"I'm still working on that." Sarah shrugged. "But she's the right age to be his mother, and he's as good a suspect as any."

Helen thought of the fellow in the fedora who'd led Bernie Winston out of the thicket when the poor man had wandered. He looked like he wanted to be a hero, not the bad guy.

She let out a slow breath. "Did you discuss this with Frank? Surely the town council vetted Mr. Danielson before they hired him?"

"According to Bertha Beaner, they had such a bunch of losers interview that Danielson seemed a shining star," Sarah said. "They hired him on the spot."

"Without a background check?"

"This is River Bend, Helen, not the big city," the other woman reminded her. "People don't expect to get taken for a ride around here. They're so trusting half the town still keeps their doors unlocked."

Helen nodded. She was right about that.

"If he's squeaky-clean, then he'll have nothing to worry about when I snoop around his apartment in the Historical Society," Sarah went on to say.

"Snoop?" Helen wasn't sure how she was going to accomplish that feat. "Mr. Danielson has suspended tours of the museum and blocked volunteers from working on current projects indefinitely, until the flood's subsided."

"Convenient for him, isn't it?" Sarah smiled slyly. "Well, that might keep regular folks away, but not me. Besides, I don't need him to let me in, do I?" She reached into her other jacket pocket and withdrew a familiar silver key ring, the spare the sheriff kept for the Historical Society.

"You're going to break in?"

"It's not breaking in if I have the key."

"What if he catches you?"

Sarah's eyes glinted. "I had my cousin Jana call Mr. Danielson pretending to be a curator at the Missouri History Museum in St. Louis. She told him they want to discuss borrowing some of River Bend's artifacts for an exhibit on Mississippi River Valley myths. By the time Danielson gets there, finds out it's a ruse, and comes back, I'll have had at least two hours to poke around."

"Does Frank know what you're up to?" Helen asked, feeling sorry for the sheriff. He had enough on his hands with Bernie Winston's death and Betty Winston practically accusing a con man named Jackson Lee of having something to do with it.

"Don't worry about Frank. I'll fill him in when I've got something concrete on John Danielson," Sarah said and pocketed the key ring. "If he's the Mr. Maybe I'm looking for, I'm going to take him down, Helen, wait and see. Then the whole town will have to admit they were wrong about Luann and I was right."

With that, she sidestepped Helen as she walked away, hopped into her Jeep, and rumbled off.

# Chapter 24

AFTER FRANK DROPPED off Betty Winston so she could mourn with her kin, he went back to his office and spent a good hour or more hunched over the computer on his desk. His main focus: delving into the background of Jackson Lee, the fellow Betty Winston claimed had been harassing Bernie in an attempt to defraud him.

He'd suspected the name might be an alias; but apparently it was real.

His full name was Jackson David Lee, and he had a valid Illinois driver's license that described him as six feet tall and 175 pounds with blue eyes and brown hair. He had an address in downtown Alton, which Frank hoped was still current. He zoomed in on the DMV photograph and thought the fellow looked younger than his fifty-two years, not bad-looking either, with a straight nose and devilish grin.

There was a single car registered in his name: a black 2005 Cadillac DeVille.

That jibed with the vehicle Betty Winston said she'd seen outside their house on more than one occasion.

Frank hit a couple more keys, pulling up current warrants and finding none for Jackson David Lee, although he did have a tidy little rap sheet, mostly involving misdemeanors on the order of stealing unsigned checks, kiting checks, trespassing, and even misrepresenting his identity on an Internet dating site.

It appeared that any charges had merely resulted in fines, which were promptly paid. Mr. Lee had no jail time to his credit, so far as Frank could discern.

Still there were questions that banged like a drum in the back of the sheriff's mind, such as whether or not Jackson Lee had been hanging around the Winstons' place hoping to bamboozle an incapacitated Bernie, or worse, if he'd had anything to do with Bernie getting out of the house and ending up in the creek last night. Had Mr. Lee tried to enter the Winston residence? Had he inadvertently let Bernie out? Would that explain why Bernie had Mr. Lee's pen in his pocket?

But there was something more.

Was Jackson Lee the Jackie that the neighbor, Ezra Bick, said was Penny Tuttle's son? Had Luann's car truly been in the Tuttles' garage when Sarah had been poking around with Helen Evans the day before? If so, where was it now? Had Jackie moved it, afraid that they were onto him?

Was he responsible in any way for Luann Dupree's sudden vanishing act?

The sheriff felt a little like he was trying to add two plus three to get four. Though he reminded himself that piecing together an investigation often felt like that at first.

By all appearances, Luann had run off with a fellow she'd met in an Internet chat room or some such place. What if Jackson had misrepresented himself to her, conned her, and then tucked her away somewhere safe so she couldn't turn him in? He seemed long overdue for a stint behind bars. He'd gotten off easy so far, but if Luann had decided to press charges—and she seemed like a tough enough lady to do it—Jackson would have been screwed.

Frank thought of Sarah's misty eyes, her voice pleading as she'd said, "My friend needs my help, and I need yours."

Aw, hell.

He rubbed his jaw.

He wanted to believe his wife had seen what she'd claimed she'd seen. It wasn't that he mistrusted her, but he knew she sometimes veered toward hyperbole in order to get her message heard. He'd told Sarah before that he would not use his job to check up on people for her and that his access to state law enforcement databases was strictly for professional purposes. But now it wasn't just Sarah nagging about something amiss. Frank's own gut was nagging at him.

So he dug a little bit deeper in his efforts to connect Jackson Lee with Margaret "Penny" Tuttle, delving into her records. Mrs. Tuttle was a seventy-two-year-old widow who did not have a valid Illinois driver's license. He found her Belleville address was three years behind on property taxes, and the house was in the name of Margaret and James Tuttle, listed as h/w, husband and wife. There appeared to be a lien on the place by a local roofer, but Frank could otherwise find nothing that suggested Mrs. Tuttle had been in trouble with the law. She might have financial problems, but so did a lot of people these days.

Frank would need a warrant to get any more information, and he didn't think he had probable cause, not yet.

"Nothing's ever how it looks," he murmured to himself, leaning back in his chair with a sigh. He rubbed his eyes, figuring he needed to head down the River Road to Alton and track down Jackson Lee. Despite it being a high-tech age, sometimes a good old-fashioned talking-to was the best way to get to the bottom of everything.

The phone at his desk rang, and Frank scooped it up.

"Sheriff Biddle here," he said.

The voice at the other end wasn't a familiar one. But it got his attention.

"Hey there, Sheriff, my name's Andy Bingham, and I work patrol in downtown Alton."

Frank sat up straighter. "How can I help you, Officer?"

"We found an abandoned car in a vacant lot near the Amtrak station this morning. The keys were in the ignition, and it was missing vital parts, including all four tires, rims, battery, and plates. It appears to be a late-model Fiat Spider," Bingham told him. "It's bright red."

Frank nearly choked.

"We traced the VIN to a woman named Luann Dupree. She lists her address as 123 Main Street in River Bend. She had a decal on her window for your town's Historical Society. You know who she is?"

"Oh, I know her all right," Frank said.

"Can you tell her we're towing her car to the impound lot sometime today?"

"That's a little easier said than done," Frank confessed.

"Ah, is she on vacation or something?" Bingham asked. "Seems strange she didn't file a report for a stolen car."

Not so strange, Frank mused, since no one in town had seen Luann Dupree in about a month. Maybe there was more to the story than he and the town council had been led to believe.

Briefly, he explained the situation to the officer, telling him, "I'm heading your way right now," before he hung up and grabbed his hat.

## Chapter 25

---

HELEN NOTICED THE water seemed the slightest bit lower on her frog boots as she slogged across Jersey Avenue toward the little bridge over the creek at Springfield. At least that was good news, wasn't it? Soon the streets would be dry again—albeit muddy—and life could get back to normal.

Yet that bright thought wasn't enough to cheer her as she trudged toward the Winstons' house to check in with Clara and see what she could do to help the family.

Though Betty had insisted she was fine, Helen was sure that wasn't true. She remembered the numbness that had set in after Joe died. For weeks, she had put herself on autopilot, dealing with doctors and the mortuary and lawyers, taking phone calls from friends and relatives, reading the sympathy cards that began pouring into the mailbox. It wasn't until after the memorial service, when she, her grown children, and her grand-children had taken Joe's ashes to the mausoleum, that it had hit her that he was dead.

Then she'd been inconsolable. Her physician had prescribed medication, but Helen hadn't wanted to take it. She needed to feel the loss, to go through her own grief. It was harder than anything she'd done in her life.

Betty had been married to Bernie for sixty-odd years.

She was *not* fine. She would not *be* fine again, not for a long while.

Deep in her thoughts, Helen passed the first two houses nearest the bridge without seeing them. She'd nearly gone by a third when she heard someone call her name, and she turned her head as a screen door swung open then closed with a slap.

She paused, staring up at the pristinely maintained Victorian, painted peach with dark-green-and-white gingerbread trim, that belonged to Agnes March.

"Yoo-hoo!" Her friend waved as she strode up the brick paver pathway toward the soggy sidewalk. "Got a minute?"

She smiled absently as Agnes approached, looking as smart as her cottage. She had on a crisp white blouse with a patterned scarf tied nattily at her throat, and her flat-front tan pants were tucked neatly into black knee-high Wellies.

Helen felt wrung out and wrinkled, wearing the same sweatsuit she'd had on the day before and her grimy-looking frog boots. Maybe she should have showered and changed before heading toward the Winstons', she thought, a little too late.

"I heard about Bernie," Agnes said before Helen even greeted her. "It's a horrible thing. Seems like we've had our share of losses lately, haven't we?"

"I guess we have," Helen said, thinking that a town filled with mostly old folks could hardly avoid it. But it never got any easier.

"Are you headed over to Betty's?"

"Yes."

"I need to go pay my respects, too," Agnes said, "but I thought I'd wait a little bit. I've got a coffee cake baking that I can take in the morning."

Helen nodded. "I'm sure they'll appreciate your thoughtfulness."

"It's good Betty has Clara," Agnes remarked. "The sisters are so close, despite their age difference." She glanced toward the Winstons' place a few houses down. "Did you know my family's home sat across the street from Clara's when we were growing up?"

"No," Helen replied truthfully. Clara had never mentioned it.

"Those girls sure went through the wringer when they lost their father. Their mother married a rough sort who drank a lot more than he worked. Betty left right after high school, and Clara gained so much weight. She just seemed so sad and closed off. I'm not sure if she missed her dad or her big sister more."

Helen thought of the photograph she'd found at the Historical Society, of Clara's family, all of them looking rather grim. "Was Clara mistreated by her stepfather?" she dared ask, since Agnes was a friend and not as prone to gossip as some.

Agnes pursed her lips, seeming to weigh her answer before she said, "I don't know what happened inside that house, but I do remember how Clara changed, and it wasn't just her figure. She missed curfews a lot, even ran away from home, and her mother didn't know what to do with her. I honestly think she was relieved when Clara went to stay with Betty and Bernie."

"Clara must have been hurting."

"She was. But I figure the time away was good for her," Agnes said, nodding. "When she came back to River Bend after a year gone, she seemed her old self again. She was happier, lighter somehow."

"Perhaps she needed time with her sister so she could heal."

"Perhaps," Agnes agreed, but there was something in her face, something that suggested she wasn't sharing all she recalled about Clara's sad home life way back when.

"I should go," Helen said, though Agnes caught her arm.

"I ran into Sarah Biddle yesterday, and she seemed more convinced than ever that Luann Dupree isn't gal-livanting across the country with her mystery man. I've been hoping to get word from Luann myself, and now that new director, John Danielson, has been by asking questions about Luann and if she left anything with me that belongs to the Historical Society." Agnes shrugged. "I really don't know what to say."

"I don't have any more news about Luann," Helen told her earnestly, because she wasn't big on passing off fiction as facts. "I'm sorry, but I'm as in the dark as you."

"I just don't know if I feel like I can trust Mr. Danielson."

"Trust him with what?"

"He's asked on several occasions what certain items are worth, and I've told him that it doesn't matter, as none of the current exhibits or additional items donated to the Historical Society are for sale."

"Does he want to sell things?" Helen asked. "Or is he just trying to gauge what's there, because he's responsible for it all now? Maybe he needs appraisals for insurance purposes."

"I hope it's the latter," Agnes said and screwed up her face. "I hope he takes as much care with the collections as Luann did, that's all." She patted Helen's arm. "I've got to get back to my coffee cake. Do tell Clara and Betty that they have my heartfelt sympathy, and I'll be dropping by in the morning."

"I will." Helen touched her friend's hand before she let go.

As she walked up the sidewalk toward the Winstons' place, she heard voices and the creak of the porch swing.

When she climbed the front steps, she saw Ellen and Sawyer.

Though Ellen's eyes looked puffy and red, she wasn't crying now. The swing moved back and forth gently as she engaged in silly chatter with her preteen daughter. Sawyer stuck out her tongue, then Ellen stuck out her tongue, and Sawyer shook her head, laughing.

Helen stopped on the porch and said, "That's a lovely sound to hear today."

The swing ceased its gentle swaying.

Ellen looked up. "Oh, hi, Mrs. Evans. Sawyer challenged me to roll my tongue, which I proudly admit I can do even though my offspring can't." She grinned. "Guess you didn't inherit that trick, sweetie."

"Aunt Clara can do it," Sawyer announced, "but Grandma can't."

"Ah, that's good to know," Helen said, smiling at the child before she fixed her gaze on Ellen. "How's everyone doing?"

"About as well as you'd imagine," Ellen said, and the light left her eyes. "I know we've all been gearing up for this day, considering Dad's been going downhill lately, but it's still a shock when it happens."

"I'm glad Betty has you," Helen told her. "And you, too, Sawyer."

"Grandpa's in heaven now," the child said matter-of-factly. "I woke up last night, and I saw him with the angels."

"You did?" Helen glanced at Ellen, who put an arm around Sawyer's shoulders.

The child nodded. "It was very dark, but I could see them. They looked all flowy, kind of like ghosts."

"That's reassuring, isn't it," Helen said, "to know your grandpa wasn't alone in the end?"

"That's what my mom thought, too."

"It's true," Ellen remarked, her voice catching. She ruffled her daughter's hair. "Thanks for coming by, Mrs. Evans. My mother and aunt are inside. Feel free to go on in. Sawyer and I are going to hang out here for a while. The fresh air is doing me good."

"I'll bet it is."

Helen started for the door as the pair began pushing at the porch floor again with their feet, setting the swing to swaying, its chains creaking mournfully.

As Ellen suggested, she let herself in. Quickly, she shucked her damp boots on the interior mat. Hearing Clara's voice arguing with Betty, she headed toward the noise.

"You need to lie down," Clara was saying. "Bernie would want you to take care of yourself. He wouldn't want you to punish yourself."

"I have to do something . . ."

"I can wash Bernie's bedclothes. It's not like anyone's coming by tonight, checking for dirty laundry . . ."

"Hello?" Helen said as she padded down the hallway in stocking feet. She peered through the door into a bedroom, spotting the two sisters at the foot of a double bed.

"There you are," she said, and they swung about, wide-eyed. "I ran into Ellen outside, and she told me to come in."

Clara glanced at Betty then hurried over to Helen. "Of course!" she chirped. "You're welcome anytime. We're just setting things to rights. Betty's ready to strip Bernie's bed, and I told her to go rest."

"How about if I strip the bed, and you both go sit down," Helen volunteered, waving away Clara's protests. "It's no problem. I'd like to make myself useful."

Betty said nothing. Her face appeared pinched, her eyes glazed.

"If you're sure it's all right," Clara said, taking Betty by the arm. Her sister didn't seem so inclined to go. "Helen's on our side, Betts."

Betty stood and watched for a moment as Helen set about pulling bed linens down. She folded back the comforter first and then yanked out the top sheet.

"I'll be done in a jiffy," Helen said over her shoulder. "I've done this, oh, about a million or so times."

She hummed while wrestling with the fitted sheet, which had been tucked tightly under the mattress. When she got it off and turned around, the sisters were gone.

She bundled the sheets together, dropping them

into a pile on the floor. Then she reached for the nearest pillow and started to remove the case. She paused, noting delicate stitching within the end band. Someone had embroidered half a dozen butterflies in pretty spring colors. Was that Betty's handiwork?

Helen's chest tightened, imagining Bernie falling asleep on such a lovely pillowcase last night, only to awaken for whatever reason and wander outside.

Her gaze drawn to the door across the room, she held the pillow to her chest and went nearer. Through the open blinds that covered inset glass, she could see the back deck. Was this how Bernie had gotten out? Had someone left it unlocked, or had Bernie managed to unlock it himself?

Squinting out, she spotted the back lawn, or where grass would have been if it weren't underwater. She envisioned Bernie fumbling his way to the outdoors, confused by a dream or by his own tortured brain. Had he waded into the creek without knowing what he was doing? Had the current tugged him off his feet? Had he not remembered how to swim?

It was no wonder Betty was punishing herself, as Helen had heard Clara remark. The poor woman probably felt like it was her fault that Bernie had gone outside in the dark while the whole house slept.

Helen had felt as guilty when Joe had died, even though there wasn't a dad-blamed thing she could have done to keep his heart from giving out.

She had relived that nightmare in her head at least a

million times since, always trying to imagine what she could have done to make things come out differently.

In the end, it didn't matter.

Dead was dead.

And not even a million what-ifs could change it.

## Chapter 26

THE SHERIFF SPENT a good forty-five minutes with the officer from the Alton PD who'd found Luann Dupree's abandoned Fiat. Despite the car's red paint, he could barely see it. The missing tires left the body sinking in sodden earth and buried in the knee-high weeds that surrounded it. What a great spot to ditch a vehicle, he thought, close to the highway and the Amtrak station but almost invisible.

Frank wondered if it had been stolen in the first place, as Bingham had suggested, or if Sarah was right that it had been hidden by Luann's abductor—her supposed online boyfriend—while he'd sent text messages and e-mails pretending to be Lu.

Had the fellow been after Luann's money? Why else would he take her? And why take her car, too? Maybe he'd arranged to meet her at some predetermined destination, like Penny Tuttle's house, which made sense if the alleged perpetrator was really Penny's son. Had he put something in her drink and drugged her, then held her captive and stored her car in the garage until he could decide what to do with it?

From what Sarah had told him about Mrs. Tuttle—and what the neighbor had implied—the woman was pretty much out of it. Her son, Jackie, held the reins.

Had he kept Luann in Mrs. Tuttle's house right under her nose?

But, again, what was the motive?

Sarah had blathered on about there being some kind of monumental discovery that Luann had made during the Historical Society's renovation. But when Frank had pressed her, his wife admitted it was merely a guess. Was there truly a rare object that Luann had unearthed?

Or was it all just a wild-goose chase?

For all Frank knew, Luann was having a ball with her lover, road-tripping across the country and not giving a second thought to anyone back in River Bend. The mayor and town council thought as much. No one seemed to question the e-mail allegedly sent by Luann telling them she'd resigned and asking that her last paycheck be electronically deposited.

So why should Frank question it?

Except that his wife's instincts said otherwise. And as much as he wanted to discount female intuition, Frank had learned the hard way that it was often right.

". . . with the highway a hop, skip, and jump away,

I figure he brought the car here, stripped the parts he wanted, and had a buddy pick him up," Officer Bingham was saying as Frank brought his head back into the game. "Or he could have picked off the car from the Amtrak lot. Could be that's where Ms. Dupree departed for her open-ended trip?"

"Sounds plausible enough," Biddle said, because it was, although he suspected things may have gone down a bit differently. "This might seem out of left field, but are you familiar at all with a man named Jackson Lee?"

Officer Bingham smiled tightly. "So you've met Jack, have you?"

"No, not yet," Frank told him. "But I thought I'd drop by his address after I leave here. It would appear he's been hanging around River Bend, trying to make a buck off some of our older folk."

Bingham shook his head. "He's a piece of work. He calls himself a salesman, but he's a con man. You're right that he likes to target the white-hairs. We've brought him in a couple times after complaints that he deposited checks that weren't signed. He called 'em 'demand drafts,' said they were perfectly legit because he had signed contracts." The officer shrugged. "When he produced the paperwork and the signatures were verified, we didn't have much to go on. It was a lot of 'he said/he said,' which is torture to prosecute."

"He might have done the same to a man named Bernie Winston who had Alzheimer's," Frank said.

Bingham grunted. "Is the fellow fit to press charges?"

"At this point he's not fit for anything," Biddle explained. "He's dead."

"Sorry to hear that," the officer said. "You figure Jack was involved somehow? I mean, he's a huckster, for sure, but I don't peg him as the violent type."

"It looks like Winston drowned in floodwaters, but the decedent's wife said she saw Mr. Lee's car parked out front last night when her husband disappeared, and an item purportedly belonging to Mr. Lee was found in the victim's pocket. So I figured I'd talk to Mr. Lee about it."

"You need assistance?" Bingham asked.

"Not necessary, but thanks for the offer." Frank touched the bill of his cap and tipped it appreciatively.

As he departed, the officer pressed his card into Frank's palm, reminding him, "Give me a shout when you hear from Ms. Dupree. We'll hold her car at the impound lot until she turns up."

"Will do."

Frank hoped that would be soon, if only to settle a lot of unanswered questions and get his wife to stick closer to home again.

He sidled into his black-and-white and drove a short distance to a small house not far from downtown Alton that Jackson Lee had listed as his residence on his driver's license. His rental was the second floor. Frank had looked it up on Zillow, so he knew the place the moment he saw it. It was a one-bed, one-bath, no-pets, and no-amenities kind of deal. But at four hundred bucks a month, he hadn't expected the Taj Mahal.

An older-model black DeVille sat out front by the curb, so Frank figured he was in luck. It looked like Jackson was home.

The sheriff climbed the steps to knock on the up-stairs unit designated 1B, hardly surprised when he saw the curtains part in a nearby window. A face peered out, remaining just long enough to get a good look at him before the curtains swayed closed.

He waited, but nothing happened.

"Mr. Lee, please open up," Frank said, leaning nearer the door. "It's Sheriff Biddle from River Bend. I'd like to talk to you about Bernie Winston."

More silence followed.

"Mr. Winston died sometime between last night and this morning, and his wife thinks you had something to do with his death," the sheriff added loudly enough so the man could have heard him from any of the tiny rooms within. Heck, the tenant downstairs had prob-ably heard him.

Quickly enough, the door came open, though Biddle was hardly invited in.

Instead Jackson Lee stood firmly between door and jamb. "Are you here to arrest me, Sheriff?"

"No, sir," Biddle told him. "I just have a few questions."

"I'm sorry to hear that Bernie's dead," Jackson said. Beneath shoe polish–black hair, his brow wrinkled.

"Why would that battle-ax wife of his think I had something to do with it?"

"She claims your car was parked outside their house last night, and something of yours was found in Bernie's pajama pocket." Frank had brought the pen with him, zipped up in the baggie Doc had handed over this morning. He plucked it from his trouser pocket and unfurled it so Jackson could see.

The man looked about to have a heart attack. "Hallelujah! It's my Cartier pen. I've been dying to get that baby back." He reached for it, but Frank jerked it away. He rolled up the baggie and tucked it back into his pants pocket. "C'mon, now, Sheriff, don't be that way. Can I have it, please?"

"Nope."

"But it's my lucky pen."

"Maybe it's not that lucky," Frank told him, "since it ended up in the pocket of a dead man. How'd he get it?"

Jackson sighed. "I may have left it behind when I was over at the house a while back. Bernie used it to sign a contract to invest in a piece of land . . ."

"He had end-stage Alzheimer's. What made you think he even knew what he was doing?"

"I'm not a doctor. I don't diagnose people before I do business with them."

"You didn't need a medical degree to know Bernie Winston was mentally impaired," Frank said, trying hard to rein in his temper.

"Look"—Jackson licked his lips—"I'd just like my

pen back. I'll rip up the damned contract if that's what that witch wants. But I wasn't anywhere near River Bend last night, and I've got the witnesses to prove it."

"I'm listening."

"I was at my usual Tuesday-night poker game with the boys. It was at Fred Birdsong's place up on the bluff." When he didn't seem to get the reaction he wanted, Jackson sniffed. "C'mon, Sheriff, everyone in a fifty-mile radius has heard the commercials." He cleared his throat and sang, "*You Can't Go Wrong with Birdsong.* Yes, *that* Fred Birdsong. He owns the biggest used-car dealership in Jerseyville. I was there until dawn, drinking and shooting the bull. You can ask him yourself."

"I'll do that," Biddle said, though he'd dealt with enough used-car salesmen in his day—professionally and otherwise—to know they were a smooth-talking bunch. So he had a feeling Jackson's alibi would be confirmed. Whether it was true or not was another matter entirely.

"If you don't mind my asking, what happened to Bernie?" Jackson said.

"He was found in the creek," was all the sheriff would let on. "Cause of death is still up in the air until Doc Melville looks him over and signs off."

"So he drowned?" Jackson shook his head. "What a sad way to go."

"Aren't they all," Biddle remarked. Then he asked a question that had nothing to do with Bernie Winston, but fishing was one of his favorite sports. So he gave it a shot. "You know a woman named Luann Dupree?"

Dark eyebrows arched. "Should I?"

Jackson Lee had admitted to being a poker player, so could be he was just good at lying. But Frank sensed his ignorance wasn't faked.

"Have you ever been called Jackie?" he asked.

Jackson laughed. "I've been called a lot worse."

Frank felt like he was getting nowhere. "Is your mother named Penny Tuttle?"

"Which one?"

"Excuse me?" Biddle wasn't sure what that meant.

"I had about five so-called mothers at various points of my childhood," Jackson explained. "I was a foster kid, kicked around like a hot potato from the time I was four, but none of 'em was named Tuttle, not that I can recall."

"All right, I get the picture," Frank said, not sure where else to go. He didn't have a thing to pin on him that would stick.

"I'm still not under arrest?"

"No."

*Not yet,* Frank thought.

Jackson smiled thinly. "Then I think our little chat is over, Sheriff. Have a nice day," he said and started to shut the door.

Frank pressed a palm to the door to keep it open. "Whoa, hold on. Did I just hear a scream?" he said, because he did hear a voice or voices, coming from the back of the apartment. It was as good an excuse as any to poke a nose in.

While Jackson sputtered in protest, Frank shouldered his way into the apartment, glancing around the tiny front room. He walked toward a dining table that was slathered with postmarked mail. Looked like bills with the little plastic windows. Frank picked up a few pieces, but they weren't addressed to Jackson Lee.

"What do you think you're doing?" the man asked, striding over to the sheriff and scooping the mail into a pile in his arms. "You don't have a warrant to search—"

"I don't need one if I think someone's in danger," Frank cut him off and strode toward a closed door and opened it to find the bathroom.

"There's no one else here. I'd call the police on you, except you are the police."

Frank ignored him, opening the only other closed door next.

"Hey, that's my bedroom! It's private," the fellow sputtered over his shoulder.

"There's that screaming again," the sheriff said then turned the knob and went in.

A television on the dresser was on, turned to a game show where the contestants whooped and hollered.

"You're right. No one's here. Must have been the TV," he said.

Still, he gave the room a slow once-over, spotting a couple boxes from OfficeMax sitting on the desk beside a printer that had what looked like blue paper in its feed.

Jackson edged around him, leaning against the desk and blocking Frank's view. "Are you satisfied, Sheriff? There's no one in danger."

Luann Dupree wasn't there. That was for sure. There wasn't anywhere for her to hide, unless Jackson had her squished into an itty-bitty closet. He didn't see any signs of another inhabitant: one toothbrush in the bathroom, one dirty glass and dish on the countertop, and one dented pillow on the bed.

"If I have more questions, I'll be in touch," Frank said, brushing past the man on his way out of the apartment.

He shut the door behind him, sure that Jackson Lee watched him through the window as he went down the wooden steps.

When he got to his patrol car, he made a call to Officer Bingham.

"I just paid a visit to your local huckster, Jackson Lee," he said. "Thought you might be interested to know he's got a bucketful of stolen mail, and there's a printer set up with check stationery and a carton of magnetic ink."

The supplies of a thief in the business of check fraud.

"Thanks for the tip, Sheriff."

"My pleasure."

Jackson Lee probably didn't have a thing to do with Bernie Winston's fatal drowning. Why nudge a man toward death's door when you still saw him as a meal ticket?

Frank was equally doubtful that he'd fauxmanced Luann Dupree to pilfer her bank account, but he was clearly up to no good.

It made him feel better to think ol' Jackson Lee might finally see the other side of prison bars. So far as Frank was concerned, cockroaches had nothing on swindlers.

## Chapter 27

HELEN STAYED AT the Winston house for nearly two hours, until Clara mentioned wanting to go home to check on her cats. Ellen and Sawyer were staying over with Betty, so Helen figured it was a good time to leave them alone.

She heard her cell phone ring in her warm-up pocket as she slogged through the puddles on Springfield. One glance at the number on the screen, and she sighed.

It was Sarah Biddle.

Helen let it go to voice mail.

She didn't mean to be rude. It was just that she was pretty worn out emotionally. Besides, there wasn't a good place to pause and take the call. The green wooden benches deposited here and there in the grass now stood in brown pools of water.

The river couldn't go down soon enough, she thought

as she trudged home through the muck. She left her frog boots just inside the porch door and padded into the house in her stocking feet.

Amber had heard her come in and meowed, wending round and round her ankles before Helen realized she was late to feed him lunch. She opened a fresh can of Fancy Feast and set it down for him in the kitchen. Once she'd filled a cup with cold water and drunk about half, she felt better, like if she sat down for a few minutes she might catch her second wind.

She settled on the wicker sofa, feeling the lump in her jacket pocket as she set her hands in her lap.

Reluctantly, she retrieved her cell phone and stared at it.

If she were the smart old bird everyone thought she was, she would have put it away in a drawer and ignored it. Surely whatever Sarah Biddle had to say could wait. But her curiosity got the better of her. *Might as well get it over with,* she told herself, dialing into the voice mail system and hitting the button for Speaker.

"You have one new message," it told her before she heard Sarah Biddle's voice, which came at her in a breathless rush.

"John Danielson is a dirty rotten scoundrel! You know what I saw in Lu's old apartment? Boxes slapped with mailing labels for addresses all over the place! I pried one open and found a piece of pottery that looks centuries old. There's an invoice that says it's a Native American burial bowl. He's selling it for a thousand dollars! It still has a tiny pink numbered sticker on the bottom that Luann used to tag items she inventoried, and there are a dozen more boxes ready to mail at least. Helen, he's stealing stuff that belongs to the Historical Society and putting it on eBay!"

*Good Lord.*

Had Sarah truly stumbled upon evidence of a crime? Helen listened again just to be sure she'd heard right.

Then she dialed back Sarah's number.

It rang only once before she heard the sheriff's wife exclaim, "Helen! You got my message?"

"Yes, and I truly hope you're reading this wrong. What if Danielson is selling items to raise money for the Historical Society . . ."

"Ha!" Sarah balked. "Then why wouldn't he have notified the town council about selling off the collection to raise funds? And why does it show payment was made to him and not to the RBHS? Guess what he's using as the return address."

Helen had a sinking feeling. "Not Penny Tuttle's house?"

"Bingo!"

"All right, I believe you! But I think you've done enough snooping on your own," Helen said, her heart pounding. "The sheriff needs to get involved at this point. This isn't something you can handle."

"I'm done with the apartment," Sarah said. "And I've already glanced over the display cases in the museum, and I didn't notice anything gone. He wouldn't be so stupid as to pilfer from the exhibits, since too many residents have already viewed them and taken pictures. I've got maybe twenty minutes before Danielson comes back, so I'm going down to the basement."

Helen rose to her feet, feeling like an angry mom whose child was determined to disobey. "Sarah, you listen to me! If Danielson is stealing from the Historical Society, the sheriff needs to know. You could mess things up if you keep this up."

"Frank's gone," Sarah replied. "He had to check out something in Alton."

*"No,"* Helen moaned.

"There's no time to waste." Sarah pressed the issue. "If Danielson has Lu . . . if she's still okay . . . then he's got her in the basement. Lu kept it locked because it freaked her out to go down there, and Danielson had to know that. The contractor didn't touch it during the renovation except to move the HVAC equipment upstairs, so it's still a bunch of closed-off old rooms that the hotel mostly used for storage. It would be the perfect place to stash her."

"It's probably flooded down there," Helen reminded her. "It's not safe."

But Sarah rattled on. "I'm guessing he kept her at his mom's house and then moved her here when he took her job. If he was drugging her, he could have smuggled her over in the dark in a moving box or wrapped up in a bedspread, and no one would have been the wiser."

Helen got a chill up her spine.

Was John Danielson a kidnapper as well as a thief?

She hated to think the man who'd played the hero bringing Bernie Winston safely out of the woods was really the bad guy, but it wasn't looking good.

"So John Danielson is Mrs. Tuttle's son, Jackie?"

"It makes sense, doesn't it? Just because his last name is different, doesn't mean anything. She could have re-married when he was a kid, and if he wasn't adopted by his stepfather . . ."

"Okay, okay," Helen interjected, "how about we let Frank figure it out?"

"Frank can have Danielson once I find Luann! I just can't stop now, knowing she could have been down in the basement for weeks."

She set the phone down momentarily as she re-trieved her frog boots then pulled them on. "I'm calling the sheriff and then I'm coming to get you. You'd better be outside waiting for me when I get to Main Street. You hear me, Sarah Biddle? You need to get out of there now. Danielson could come back any minute, and if he did all those things you're accusing him of, he's dangerous."

"I'm at the basement door, and it looks like the same padlock. Let's just hope he didn't rekey it," Sarah went on, as if Helen hadn't said a word. "Luann kept her key above the door threshold. I'm fishing with my fingers . . . Ah, there it is!"

"Sarah!" Helen barked. "You stop it right this minute. I'm heading out the door. If John Danielson gets you before I do, you'll be lucky."

"Hey, I'm in!" Sarah told her. "Oh, shoot, the light won't go on. You think there's water down there? Maybe it shorted the electricity. Sorry, but I'm going to have to hang up, Helen. I need to use the light on my phone until I can find the light below . . ."

"Do *not* hang up on me!"

But Helen heard nothing in response, not a breath, not a whisper, and certainly not Sarah's voice rattling on.

Her phone told her point-blank: *Call Ended.*

What in God's name did Sarah think she was doing?

Helen quickly redialed the woman's number before leaving the house, letting the screen door slap behind her.

She could hardly breathe until the ringing stopped and Sarah answered. "Don't you ever hang up on me again!" she chastised. "Where are you now?"

"I'm in the cellar. It's wet down here, but it's not too bad. There's maybe an inch or two of water. I guess the sandbagging worked. I remember seeing a light overhead right about where I'm standing. Let me swing an arm to find the chain . . . Ah, here we go!"

Helen heard a click.

"It's an awful fluorescent fixture that flickers like something from a horror film. Oh, man, is it ever creepy down here. Lu was right about the mold. It smells worse than a wet bathing suit that never dried."

"What do you see?" Helen asked, trying to focus on where she was going as she waded through the wet road.

"I see a rusted punch clock and hooks for coats or uniforms. I believe Lu told me it used to be the staff room. There's a busted-up bathroom nearby, and there's the old hotel safe."

"Surely he didn't put Luann in there," Helen said, puffing gently as she slogged through the river muck on the sidewalk, trudging toward Main Street. "The safe was meant to be airtight, wasn't it?"

"No, she's not there. The safe door's partly open. I don't think it really closes anymore," Sarah described in a quiet voice. "I can't see anything but a bunch of old empty shelves and cubbies. There are a couple of closed doors up ahead, though."

Helen listened to Sarah's loud breathing and then heard a clanging noise.

"It's kind of dark down at this end," she said, sounding spooked. "The first door's locked. Lu, are you in there!" Sarah called out, and Helen heard the noise of her pounding. "I can't get in. The second door is locked, too. Dammit!"

"Okay, enough," Helen said, finally reaching the block where the business district started and the residential area stopped. "We need to bring in the sheriff. This is ridiculous! I'm almost to you, Sarah. Come on out of there. We'll wait for Frank and go back in with him and maybe Art Beaner and Henry Potter, too."

"I've got a screwdriver. Frank gave me these tiny ones to keep on my key ring. I'll try to pry these old doors open, and if I can't, I'll take them off their hinges. But I'll need both hands. I'm going to put away my phone now. If Danielson shows up before I'm done, stall him."

*Stall him?*

"Are you nuts?" Helen croaked.

"Didn't Frank deputize you?"

"Yes, but . . ."

"Well, if you have to arrest Danielson, do it! I'm hanging up now."

"Sarah? Don't you dare . . . ," Helen demanded, only to see *Call Ended* on her screen.

*Argh.*

She paused as she reached Main Street, cursing Sarah as she caught her breath. *Enough is enough,* she decided as she dialed the sheriff's cell phone.

It took a few rings for him to answer, but when he did, she started in, "Your wife's gotten herself in a fix again! She took your key to the Historical Society and broke into the director's apartment! She had a friend lure John Danielson away, but he's due back any minute, and he's been stealing things. She found real proof this time! And she's still snooping in the dark basement, looking for Luann!"

"Whoa, Mrs. Evans," he said, sounding so far away, "what things did he steal?"

"Sarah said he's taken artifacts that Luann inventoried but weren't on display, and he's selling them to the highest bidder!"

He started to speak, but Helen ran right over him, saying, "She's convinced that Luann's being kept in the basement against her will. I wish I could tell you that Sarah's off her rocker, but I'm starting to believe her. I'm nearly at the Society building now. You've got to get here pronto!"

"I'm on the road," he told her. "I've just left Alton, and I'll need to cut through Elsah and come in via the back road. It'll be another twenty minutes at least, fifteen if I put on my siren."

"Then do it," Helen said, her heart racing.

"Don't you do anything rash," Biddle instructed. "Wait outside until I get there. Don't put yourself in danger, too."

But Helen didn't hang on to listen.

She pocketed her phone, pressed onward, up the messy sidewalk, past the Closed signs in the windows of the Cut 'n' Curl and Agnes's antiques shop, until she reached the door to the Historical Society just as a black Ford Explorer pulled up in front.

Wasn't that John Danielson's car?

Helen swallowed.

If things weren't bad enough already, they were about to get worse.

## Chapter 28

HELEN WATCHED THE vehicle park in the watery street. Danielson got out and slogged to the sidewalk, his Dockers tucked into the tops of black rain boots. He had a small duffel bag slung over his shoulder, probably containing a pair of dress shoes. Helen wondered how he'd felt when he'd gotten to the Missouri History Museum only to find out his appointment there was a ruse. No wonder he was frowning.

*Lord, give me strength,* she thought and geared up for her helpless-old-lady routine.

"Why, there you are, Mr. Danielson!" she said, all aflutter. "I've been hoping I'd catch you when you weren't slashing through the jungle with your machete to save a lost citizen."

Instead of smiling at her flattery, he approached her with a scowl.

"Mrs. Evans . . ."

"Oh, goodness," she trilled. "I'm surprised you remember my name when you've probably met so many folks in River Bend that we all look alike."

She let out a little laugh that sounded fake even to her own ears, but it didn't matter. John Danielson didn't seem amused in the least.

"I thought I told you that I'd suspended volunteer work until the floodwaters receded. I haven't changed my mind."

"Well, yes, you did, but I was wondering if . . . if I might treat you to a late lunch at the diner and discuss some, er, fund-raising projects I had in mind for this year," she said, clutching hands at her chest, as much an act of prayer as nerves.

"Fund-raising projects?" he repeated and glanced toward the Historical Society door, barely ten feet away from him. Only Helen and a large puddle stood between them. "I'm sorry, ma'am, maybe another day. I really want to get back to work. I've just wasted a lot of time running into St. Louis on a fool's errand." He sighed with disgust, looking downright pissed. "I'm kind of worn out. So if you'll excuse me, I'm going inside . . ."

"Perfect!" she piped up. "I'll go in with you. I seem to have lost something, and I think I left it there in the room where Clara and I were last working on the photographs."

"What was it you lost exactly?"

*What, what, what? C'mon, Helen, think!*

"It was my . . . um, glasses," she finally got out. Her cheeks felt hot with embarrassment. "Yes, my favorite pair."

John Danielson squinted at her. "You've got your glasses on, ma'am."

Helen laughed nervously. "Oh, these?" she said and touched the bifocals perched on her nose. "They're my old standbys. I must have left my new ones here the last time Clara and I sorted photographs. I'd hate to lose them."

"I think you're mistaken," he said, "because I don't recall seeing any glasses on the table when I cleared everything out. Trust me, I'm very meticulous."

*No doubt,* Helen thought, considering how well he'd covered his tracks.

"I'm sure that's true, but it wouldn't hurt to check again, would it?" she said, adding, "Sometimes even careful folks make mistakes."

He gave her a funny look. "All right," he replied before he glanced around, the crow's-feet around his eyes deepening.

Was he making sure there were no witnesses?

Helen was relieved to see a few diehards heading into the diner across the way. But otherwise the downtown was deserted. Most of the shops were closed and signs in the watery road reminded folks that the off-ramp to the River Road was still inaccessible.

If she went inside the Historical Society and screamed, would anyone even hear?

"Come on in," the director said, "but let's make it quick."

Helen couldn't do much except move out of his way.

He had his key ready when he got to the door, but as he jabbed it in, the knob instantly turned. "What the . . . ?" he started to say. "I know I locked up."

"I do that sometimes," Helen nattered on from behind him. "I think I've locked the door, and it's open. Or I'm sure I turned off the TV, but it's still on. Sometimes I tell myself that Amber did it." She laughed nervously. "But of course, he can't, right? He's a cat."

Danielson didn't wait for Helen to enter before him. He clomped inside, not seeming to care that he trailed river water in with him. He barely paused to stomp on the interior mat before he swung his duffel aside, dumping it on the floor.

"Why are all the lights on?" he remarked as he walked through the hallway.

If he kept going, he'd see that Sarah had removed the padlock from the basement door, and the jig would be up.

*C'mon, Sheriff,* Helen thought. *Hurry!*

If only she could get her phone out and warn Sarah that they were inside. Although Helen imagined Sarah could probably hear their footsteps on the creaky old floors regardless. Surely that was warning enough.

"Maybe we should look upstairs on the second floor," Helen suggested, trying to divert him. "My glasses might be in the big room where Clara and I used to work . . ."

"No!" Danielson said, so brusquely Helen took a step back, bumping into the fire extinguisher on the wall behind her. "I would have noticed them, ma'am, when I organized the room. They're not there, I assure you."

"Okay, let's not go upstairs, then."

A heavy *thump* resonated from below and then Sarah hollered, "*Helen!* She's here! If that's you up there, please help!"

*Oh, Lord.*

Helen cringed.

"What the hell's going on?" Danielson's narrowed gaze went straight to the basement door. Not only was it ajar, but the padlock hung freely from the ring of the hasp bar screwed into the jamb. "I won't let you do this," he snarled, and reached out to grab Helen's arm.

Before he got her, Helen swiveled, pulling the fire extinguisher from the wall.

Her mind felt like mud as she tried to remember how to operate the danged thing. PASS, wasn't it? Pull pin, aim, squeeze, and sweep. But her fingers shook so badly she couldn't get the pin to come out.

Danielson caught her elbow as he threw the door open. "Get down there!" he told her, jerking her forward.

With her free hand, Helen swung the extinguisher at him as hard as she could. With a *clang* it connected with his head.

Danielson cursed her, letting her go as he stumbled backward. There was blood at his brow, which only seemed to enrage him. "You old bit—" he started to say.

But Helen took a few steps forward and hit him again.

This time he lost his footing. He cried out as he tumbled down the wooden staircase, thudding down the steps.

Her first thought: *Oh, God, have I killed him? Is he dead?*

Her second: *Screw that!*

Breathing hard, Helen dropped the extinguisher, reaching for the manual fire alarm on the wall. She grabbed the lever and pushed it down with all her might.

The alarm blasted noise through her head, and Helen sank to the floor, pressing her palms to her ears, feeling like her skull would explode.

Within a minute, she felt the vibration of feet and suddenly bodies were all around her. She looked up to see several men she didn't know and then Erma from the diner, holding hands over her ears, as well. Helen wanted to cry with relief when she spotted the sheriff, hovering above her like a big beige hound dog.

"Where's the fire?" Erma yelled through the din.

The sheriff shut off the alarm, extending his hand to Helen and helping her rise from the floor.

"I think Mrs. Evans must've already put it out," he said.

## Chapter 29

THE SHERIFF CALLED for an ambulance and then for Amos Melville.

Doc showed up in about two minutes flat with his black bag in hand. He went down to the basement with the sheriff, who told Helen to stay upstairs, keeping onlookers out and letting the paramedics in.

Sarah Biddle did not leave Luann's side for a moment. Helen later heard that she'd used her key-chain screwdriver to remove the hinges of the door that Danielson had locked. Doc surmised that Luann had been in the basement for weeks.

The woman was in pretty bad shape, often left without a light on, given enough food and water to survive but kept heavily sedated, lying upon a bare mattress set atop a wooden pallet to keep her dry from the damp concrete floor.

When the ambulance showed up to take Lu to Jersey Community Hospital in Jerseyville, Sarah had insisted on riding along with her.

Helen got a glimpse of Luann, looking dirty and drawn, her hair matted and eyes foggy. Sarah clutched her hand as the paramedics set up the gurney to roll her out. As Helen stood aside, she heard Luann whisper in a paper-thin voice, "You were right . . . It was just like a horror movie."

Sheriff Biddle had no sympathy when John Daniel-son complained of injuries from his fall down the stairs and from the growing goose egg where Helen had hit him on the head.

He arrested the man on the spot, telling him he'd haul his butt personally to Jersey Community Hospital and then happily turn him over to the good folks at the county lockup.

"I'm sure I'll find Luann's phone and laptop when I search your apartment, won't I, Mr. Danielson. You're going down for a long time, pal," Biddle insisted as he cuffed the man's arms behind his back. "Kidnapping, theft, fraud, assault, so many charges to choose from," he chided.

"I did it for my mother," Danielson said, his eyes on Helen, blood dripping from his temple. "You of all people should understand, Mrs. Evans. She's got dementia and a load of other issues. You must know how expensive it is to care for someone who's sick, what it costs to pay for help. She can't be left alone. And that stupid man she married after my father went through her savings faster than a dog through kibble! He couldn't even pay to keep up the house, and now I can't sell it because of the liens."

But Helen pursed her lips, saying nothing.

She had no sympathy for him, not after what he'd done.

*You should have reached out and asked for help,* she wanted to scream. If only he'd done that instead of looking for a victim online, for a woman willing to talk about her life and her work, thinking she'd found a soul mate, when in fact all she'd done was reel in a desperate and dangerous man.

When the ambulance had gone and the sheriff's black-and-white had departed with Danielson tossed in the back, Helen found herself alone with Doc Melville.

They stood in the front room of the Historical Society, the floor around them muddied by dozens of feet that had come and had gone. The smell of the river seeped into the air from the front door, left wide open.

But it was finally quiet after so much confusion and noise.

"She'll be okay," Doc said as Helen stood quietly, arms tightly crossed. "She'll be back here soon, right where she belongs."

Helen looked around her, at the display cases surrounding them, filled with artifacts that Luann Dupree had so painstakingly researched and catalogued and put out for all of River Bend to learn from and share.

It was clear to see how much of her heart went into this place, to preserving the past and all that had come before. To John Danielson, on the other hand, the relics were a means to an end, not to be cherished but to be sold to the highest bidder. And Luann had just stood in his way.

"It's been a hard time around here lately, hasn't it?" Amos went on. "Life is not easy sometimes, but we trudge on regardless. And at least there's a happy ending to Luann's story."

"Unlike Bernie's," Helen said, her voice hoarse. She felt strangely defeated when she should have felt buoyed after Luann's rescue. "But I guess there's no happy ending when you have Alzheimer's, is there?"

Doc said nothing. He didn't even grunt, which roused her suspicions.

"Amos?" she said, uncrossing her arms and walking toward him. "What's wrong?"

Doc looked positively ashen.

Helen had known Amos and Fanny Melville for all of the fifty years that she'd lived in River Bend. Doc had taken care of her family, her kids, and Joe when he'd gotten sick. In fact, Doc had done all a human could do to prolong her husband's life, and she loved him for it. She loved Fanny like a sister.

She could tell when he was heartbroken, and he appeared to be that. She just wasn't sure why.

"Are you okay?" she asked and jerked her chin toward a bench between display cases. "Can you sit a minute?"

She nudged him toward it, and they plunked down side by side. He put his black bag by his feet with a sigh.

"Frankly, I've been better," he said.

"It's not Fanny?" Helen asked, although she didn't think so. She'd seen her friend just the day before after Bernie's rescue, and she'd looked fine. Still, looks could be deceiving.

"No, no, Fanny's good." Doc shook his head. "It's Bernie Winston."

Helen took a stab in the dark. "You've done an exam? Is the death certificate signed so Betty can proceed with cremation?"

Doc opened his hands, palm-up, as if showing they were empty.

Helen sucked in a breath before she let it out slowly. "Something's off, isn't it? You're not satisfied."

"He had no water in his lungs," Amos said pointedly. "He couldn't have been in the water for long, or else the lungs would've been filled with water, no matter how he died."

"You can tell that without autopsy?"

"I can ascertain it well enough through palpation."

If Helen hadn't already felt like she was in *the Twilight Zone*, she would have thought it then. "Hold on a second. Are you saying that Bernie didn't drown?"

"I'm saying it's suspicious."

"Maybe he fell and hit his head before he went into the creek? That would explain the lack of water in his lungs."

"No, he didn't have any new contusions or abrasions to his skull that I could see," Amos countered. "Remember, I'd just examined him the day before when he came out of the woods. So I had a solid basis for comparison."

"Heart attack?" Helen suggested.

"He's got petechial hemorrhaging and some strange mottling around his nose and mouth. It's as though something was pressed into his skin, almost in a pattern."

"You think someone else was involved?"

"I'm saying I don't know," Doc admitted. He raised his hands to his face, touching spots around his own nose and mouth. "They were strange-looking marks, and you'll probably think I'm crazy, but they appeared to be shaped like butterflies."

"Butterflies?" Helen repeated.

Doc harrumphed. "I said you'd think I was crazy."

"No," she whispered, "sadly, I don't."

An all-encompassing weariness swept through her, a moment of epiphany that she wished she could undo by simply squishing her eyes closed. It had been a hard time lately, yes, far beyond anything she had understood until right then.

She wet her lips. "What are you going to do?" she asked.

Doc hung his head. "I don't know, Helen. I truly don't. I thought I'd talk to Frank and see if he wanted to pursue this. I could request an autopsy . . ."

"An autopsy?" Helen's pulse jumped. "Oh, Amos,

you know as well as I do that anything could have happened to Bernie. Can't we let him rest in peace? That poor family has been through enough. Isn't it time we let them move on?"

For a long moment, the doctor sat silently. He smoothed blue-veined hands over his knees, fiddled with his wedding band, until finally he cleared his throat.

"You're right, of course. I have no proof that anything happened beyond an octogenarian with Alzheimer's leaving his home in the middle of the night and ending up lifeless in the flooded creek. He could have had a fatal stroke or his advanced disease could have just told his lungs to stop breathing." Doc turned tired eyes upon Helen. "It seems a logical conclusion, wouldn't you say?"

"I would." She patted his hand. "Does that mean you're going to sign the death certificate?"

"Yes," he said and picked up his bag, rising to his feet.

"It's the right thing, Amos. It is."

"Are you sure?" He looked at her, earnestly searching for an answer.

Helen nodded, but the companionable air between them turned awkward, and she understood why. He suspected what she knew. His eyes told her that more clearly than words.

And there was nothing either of them could do to change it.

## Chapter 30

HELEN PARTED WAYS with Amos, hardly seeing as she walked. It was as though her feet knew precisely where she wanted to go, and they carried her there, without a second thought.

She had to take a few deep breaths before she went up the path to the Winstons' house, and not because she'd gone too fast. It would require a fair bit of courage to do what had to be done, but she couldn't go on if she didn't.

Helen wasn't good at pretending. She never had been, particularly not with a person she knew as well— *thought* she knew as well—as Clara.

She'd barely tapped a fist against the door before it was answered.

Her friend stood before her, meeting her eyes, as if she knew why Helen had come.

"Is your sister here?" she asked, and Clara nodded. "May I come in?"

"Sure." Her friend drew the door wide so Helen could pass.

"Is Ellen here with Sawyer?"

"No," Clara told her. "They went back into St. Louis for a few hours, but they'll return to spend the night."

"Where's Betty?"

"She's been sitting on the back porch staring out at the flooded creek for the last hour."

"I'm sure she has," Helen said.

"I heard there was some commotion downtown," Clara remarked, following behind her as Helen went through the cottage. "I got a call from Bertha Beaner. Art told her that John Danielson had been arrested, that Luann had been stuck in the basement all this time."

"It's true." Helen paused in the kitchen, seeing through to the porch and to the back of the wicker chair where Betty sat, her hair a white poof of cotton.

"So it seems that silly Sarah Biddle was right all along."

"I guess she was, yes."

Clara clicked tongue against teeth. "Sometimes things aren't what they appear on the surface."

"No, they aren't," Helen said, thinking that applied to people, too.

She turned her back on Clara and stepped out onto the porch. The sound of the water moving in the creek beyond the screens seemed so loud in its rushing. Trees hung in a canopy above the small speck of yard that was still green and not covered by muck.

Helen settled onto a bentwood chair with a hard seat. She preferred that it was uncomfortable. She hadn't come to shoot the breeze.

Clara stood in the doorway, one hand on the frame. Helen half expected her to say, "I know why you've come, and you can't do this. Go away."

But she didn't.

"Hello, Betty," Helen said, though the cottony head did not pivot in her direction. "I had a most interesting conversation with Doc Melville a few minutes ago. He's done his exam on Bernie. I'm sure you'll be relieved to hear that he's going to sign the death certificate . . ."

"Oh, thank God," Clara said, and put a hand over mouth. She started to cry, and Helen glanced over, concerned. But Clara waved her off and wandered inside.

All the better, Helen mused.

She pulled her chair closer to Betty's.

"Don't assume that Doc didn't have some serious questions about what happened to Bernie, because he did. He still does, in fact, and so do I."

Betty's chin came up a notch.

"Here's how I believe the story goes," she went on. "I think it all started many, many years ago when you were first married and Clara was just a teenager. I saw the family photograph from the Historical Society archives before Clara stuffed it in her bag. She told me about living with you and Bernie when she was sixteen.

She said you saved her life. She was pregnant then, wasn't she?"

"She's my sister," Betty said, very matter-of-factly. "She needed me."

"Was it her stepfather?" Helen asked. "Was he responsible for her condition?"

"He was a horror," Betty admitted, finally looking away from the creek and at Helen. "He was a drunk and he was cruel, but he wasn't responsible, not entirely. He made Clara's home life intolerable, but he didn't touch her, not that way. It was a boy at Clara's school, someone who took advantage of her confusion. She just gave up caring, and she let things get out of control."

The picture became so much more vivid then, mental brushstrokes filling in the missing colors in Helen's mind. What she had only suspected before seemed so logical now. "She was pregnant already when she moved in with you."

"Yes."

"Did your mother know?"

Betty's fingers tightened, clawlike, over the arms of the chair. "Clara didn't tell anyone but me. She was too afraid. She was heavy then, too, so no one guessed. Her troubles with our stepfather were enough of an excuse to get her out. Our mother didn't even try to stop her."

"Ellen is Clara's daughter, isn't she? She had the baby, and you and Bernie raised her as your own. It was all very hush-hush, I'm sure."

"Yes, very hush-hush." The words emerged as a whisper.

"Everything was fine and dandy," Helen continued, "until Bernie got Alzheimer's and started saying things, wild things, like Ellen wasn't his child. It sounded like the ravings of a madman, except to you and Clara."

"Bernie and I . . . we could never get pregnant, not in any way that lasted," Betty said, looking down. "He blamed himself, but I was sure it was me."

"I'm sorry."

Betty put her hands in her lap but said nothing.

"Ellen doesn't know, does she?"

"No."

"You were afraid she would be hurt if she realized the truth, that she'd be confused and angry that you and Clara kept it a secret."

"Yes," Betty said, choking on the word. "We had to do something. She couldn't know. It would ruin everything, and Bernie was as good as gone already."

*As good as gone.*

Not dead, but not the same man, more a burden than a companion, afflicted with an illness from which he could never recover, one that battered and bruised the caregiver, as well.

Helen gazed at the woman, her eyes exhausted and pain filled, her shoulders stooped. She might be strong of will, but not of body. She could not have done it alone, Helen knew. She may have pressed the pillow to Bernie's face, the one with the embroidered butterflies that left their shapes upon Bernie's skin; but she could not have gotten his lifeless form out the door without help.

Clara must have abetted her sister in hauling the rail-thin body to the creek and dumping him in. There was no other scenario that made sense.

*Grandpa's in heaven now. I woke up last night, and I saw him with the angels . . . It was very dark, but I could see them. They looked all flowy, kind of like ghosts.*

Sawyer had seen them: two women in their nightgowns, outside in the dark, engaged in an act of desperation. Only she hadn't known what was going on.

Her young mind—her *innocent* mind—had imagined she saw angels.

That was a good thing, Helen realized, far better than having the girl recognize that her aunt and her mother were doing a terrible thing.

"Are you going to tell the sheriff?" Betty asked.

Helen saw the distress in her face, could read it in her trembling hands. She didn't condone what the women had done, but she couldn't sic the sheriff on them either. What good would it do to lock them up? They weren't a threat to anyone.

*God help me,* Helen thought, but she couldn't make something bad even worse. Wouldn't living with what they had done be punishment enough?

"I won't turn you in."

Betty gulped, and tears streamed down her cheeks. "I love Ellen with all my heart," she sobbed, "and Sawyer, too. *They* are my all. They are my life now. It's true. It's really true."

Helen closed her eyes for a moment, not hearing Betty's voice or the rush of the creek beyond the porch screens, hearing instead Sawyer's high-pitched laughter. She thought of the girl and her mother, neither knowing the truth of Ellen's birth, neither realizing the secret that had been safeguarded with Bernie's death, and she hoped to God that she'd done the right thing.

## Chapter 31

*Monday, Two Weeks Later*

HELEN WALKED BRISKLY toward River Bend's downtown, thankful for the sidewalks that the maintenance crew had hosed down and swept clean once the flood had receded. Barely an inch of murky water remained on the street, though there was plenty of mud to go around. Plenty of litter remained, as well: brush and twigs, dead fish, and rubbish from foam cups to fenders, all waiting to be cleared away.

Piles of rotted wood and ruined carpeting accumulated on the curbs in front of the homes nearest the creek. An e-mail from the town council had gone out just that morning with the schedule for trash trucks hired to haul away the mounds of debris. The air hummed with the noise of pressure washers, and Helen spotted plenty of folks spraying sludge from siding and rinsing off their driveways.

It wouldn't be long before this latest flood was a distant memory, although Helen would surely never forget it, even though it hardly rivaled the Great Flood of '93. She doubted that Clara Foley or Betty Winston would forget it either, or Luann Dupree, though each desperately wanted to put it behind her.

*The world is full of suffering. It is also full of overcoming it.*

She thought of the Helen Keller quote printed on the calendar her granddaughter Nancy had given her for Christmas. It struck a chord in Helen and stayed with her. She reminded herself of it on days like this and realized the truth in the words.

If there wasn't hope of something more, something better, how could a person put one foot in front of the other and continue?

Helen had faith, and Luann Dupree seemed ready to embrace hope, too.

She had called Helen just the day before, inviting her to the Historical Society for "a little celebration."

"What's the occasion?" Helen had asked, though she had her suspicions. Luann had (mostly) recovered from her ordeal and had been newly restored to the position of Historical Society director. "Isn't it your first official day back at the helm?"

"That's part of it," Luann had told her. "The rest is a surprise."

"Should I bring a dish?" she asked, because that was what folks did in River Bend.

"No, don't bring a thing besides yourself," Lu had replied, which was the reason Helen headed toward the Historical Society empty-handed.

As she passed Agnes's antiques shop, the door flew open.

"Yoo-hoo!" her friend called out. "Are you heading to the Historical Society, by chance?"

"I am," Helen said, wondering how Agnes knew.

"What a coincidence. So am I," her friend said, answering the unspoken question. She asked Helen to wait while she closed up her shop; then Agnes joined her.

Helen noticed the rather large paper bag that Agnes carried. "Are you bringing a treat? Luann told me not to."

"A treat?" Agnes repeated, like the idea was too precious. "Well, I guess I am." She grinned, baring teeth not quite as shiny as the pearls at her collar.

Something funny was going on. Helen didn't need Poirot's mustache or Sherlock Holmes's deerstalker hat to figure out that much.

When they arrived at the front door of the three-story brick building, there was a sandwich-board sign that announced: *Private Event*. Anchored to it were colorful balloons that bobbed in the wind.

Helen held the door for Agnes, and they both went inside.

Light flooded the interior, illuminating the display cases and reflecting off the glass that gleamed as though freshly polished. A spotlight shone down on one case in particular, a smaller one that stood front and center in the main room of the Historical Society's museum space. It stood out for another reason, as well: it was empty. Beside it sat a tray table, though it was empty, too.

"Strange," Helen remarked. "Could this be the surprise Luann mentioned?"

"Could be," Agnes said and looked fit to giggle.

Helen frowned, feeling left out and not liking it one iota.

"Ah, good, you're here!" a voice exclaimed, and Luann Dupree entered the room, arms outstretched, a broad grin on her carefully made-up face.

Helen thought she looked rather fit after all she'd been through. A little drawn around the eyes, a little thinner, but healthy enough.

"Frank, Sarah, this way!" Luann called over her shoulder.

The sheriff and his wife appeared a few beats later, he, as ever, in uniform, while she wore a pastel striped dress and had her mousy hair tamed in a loose ponytail.

Both appeared as perplexed about the gathering as Helen.

Not one to mince words, Sarah remarked, "This is quite a small party."

"Yes, it is," Luann said. "And since everyone's here, we'll get started. Agnes?"

She turned toward the other woman, who removed a cardboard box from the bag she'd brought with her.

Agnes placed the box on the tray table then took off the lid before stepping back.

"Thank you for everything," Lu said and gave Agnes a brief hug. "I can't imagine what would have happened if you hadn't taken such great care."

"Happy to do it," Agnes said, her voice muffled against Luann's shoulder.

Helen exchanged glances with Sarah Biddle.

She'd never seen anyone hug Agnes March before. As kind as she was, Agnes wasn't exactly the touchy-feely type. She was more starch and pearls, except with Sweetum, of course, her beloved Westie.

Luann cleared her throat, regaining her composure. "While I was, um, out of commission, Agnes watched over something very important to me, very important to all of us," the Historical Society director explained as she drew a pair of white gloves from her pocket and donned them. "If Agnes hadn't kept the secret I'd asked her to keep, we might not be here today to celebrate this incredible discovery."

With gloved fingers, she reached into the box and removed a piece of tea-stained paper protected by an archival plastic sleeve.

"This," she said, holding it up for them to see, "is a page from the diary of Jacques Lerner, the fur trader who built the cabin in the woods that's been a coveted destination for every child in River Bend for as long as I've been around . . ."

"Oh, longer than that," Agnes quipped to nervous laughter.

"The journal was discovered when stored boxes were moved out of what is now the director's apartment," Luann explained. "It was left to the Historical Society by the Herbert family, who settled in the valley two centuries ago when River Bend was founded."

Helen wasn't the only one listening intently. Neither Biddle had so much as twitched.

"Let me read this page to you, though you'll have to excuse my horrible French," Luann said then stumbled through the passage: *"Et je ne pouvais pas croire ma bonne fortune quand M. Lewis m'a remercié pour avoir étendu mon hospitalité en me donnant un collier de griffe d'ours, qui lui avait été présenté par un chef Shoshone . . ."*

Helen picked up a few words here and there, enough to feel a tingle up her spine, particularly when Luann translated the passage to English.

"I could not believe my great fortune when Mr. Lewis thanked me for extending my hospitality by giving me a bear-claw necklace, which had been presented to him by a Shoshone chief."

Helen gasped, as did the sheriff.

Sarah Biddle, on the other hand, let out a whoop. "I knew it! I knew it was real!"

Luann set the page aside and reached back into the box, digging beneath the acid-free tissue to withdraw the item in question.

When she held it up, Helen's eyes went wide.

There had to be three dozen or more three- to four-inch bear claws, she surmised, tied together with leather strips. It was magnificent and strange and thrilling to see.

"It's a physical link to the past," Luann said, voice trembling with pride. "And a reminder that such a momentous event as the Lewis and Clark expedition actually touched our little town when it was hardly more than a fur-trading post along the river. I hope it will be viewed by our citizens and visitors for many years to come."

Again, Agnes stepped forward to assist, opening the glass case, in which the necklace and letter were carefully placed side by side.

"The amazing Ms. March had her friend at the Field Museum in Chicago authenticate the piece, as did an expert in American Indian studies from the University of Illinois," Lu said, closing the glass lid and locking it securely. "To think that if I hadn't given it to her when I did, it might not be here today. *I* might not be here today."

This time it was Agnes who hugged Luann. "My pleasure, sweetheart," she said.

*Drop off Sat AM.* Helen remembered the notation in the margin of the *New York Times* article Sarah had shown her, the one about the bear-claw necklace that had been misplaced for a hundred or more years at the Peabody Museum.

It hadn't meant "drop off Saturday morning," but "drop off Saturday Agnes March."

Helen watched as Agnes returned to stand beside her, looking embarrassed at the attention and fiddling with the pearls around her neck.

No wonder Agnes had said she couldn't trust John Danielson and kept asking when Luann was coming back. She'd had the necklace all along, and she'd protected it. In doing so, she'd protected Luann, as well.

Agnes caught her staring and winked.

"Congratulations, ma'am," the sheriff said, moving forward to take a look into the case. "This is quite an amazing find. You'll have to upgrade the security around here, though, and the town council will have to update the building's insurance, no doubt."

"Insurance? Phooey! Who cares about insurance?" Sarah cuffed her husband's shoulder and let out a squeal that made Helen jump. "I'm so happy for you, Lu. You deserve this! Every museum in the country is going to come after this, you know. They're going to offer you millions for it, and the newspapers will write about you like you're a superstar. We'll have a hard time keeping you in River Bend. You'll have your pick of genuine adventures . . ."

"No, thank you," Luann cut her off, tearfully looking around at her tiny museum. "I think, from now on, I'll keep my adventures close to home."

"I'm so happy to hear that! How about instead of finding a boyfriend, you get a handsome neutered cat,"

Sarah suggested, slinging an arm around her friend's shoulders. "You could name him Mr. Right."

Luann gave her a look. "Not funny!"

Sarah chuckled. "Oh, yes, it was."

"Hey, is anyone up for a cup of punch?" Agnes asked. "I think we ought to toast Luann before we cut the cake."

"Did you say cake?" The sheriff instantly perked up. "If you need someone to wield a knife, I'm your man."

"You mean, if you need someone to eat it, you're the man," Sarah tossed over her shoulder.

Yep. Helen smiled. Things were getting back to normal already.

## *Other River Road Mysteries*

### To Helen Back

*In this fun and sassy new mystery,* USA Today *bestselling author Susan McBride introduces us to Helen Evans, a modern-day Miss Marple who must expose a murderer in a town full of suspects!*

When Milton Grone turns up dead in tiny River Bend, Illinois, nearly all the would-be suspects have the perfect alibi: attending Thursday night's town meeting. And as Milton was hardly beloved, plenty of folks had a reason to do him in . . .

Grone's next-door neighbor was furious about a fence that encroached on her property, among other wicked deeds. A pair of zealous tree huggers wanted Grone's hide for selling a parcel of pristine land to a water park. Grone's current and ex-wife both wanted a cut of the profits, which Grone seemed unwilling to share. Even the town preacher knew Grone's soul was beyond saving.

Though most of River Bend would rather reward the killer than hang him, Sheriff Biddle's not about to let this one go . . . and neither is Helen Evans. With a penchant for puzzles and an ear for innuendo, Helen quickly fingers the culprit before Biddle puts the wrong suspect in jail.

# Mad as Helen

*In the second River Road Mystery from USA Today bestselling author Susan McBride, Helen Evans must find a killer before her granddaughter is arrested for murder!*

When tiny River Bend, Illinois, is hit by a string of burglaries even Sheriff Frank Biddle can't solve, the clients of LaVyrle's Cut 'n' Curl can hardly talk of anything but. There are no signs of forced entry and no fingerprints, and valuables are missing from secret hiding places, as if the thief knew what he wanted and just where to look.

Helen Evans wonders what the world has come to if even their once-quiet town isn't safe anymore. Then Grace Simpson, a big-city psychotherapist who had opened up shop in River Bend, is found dead on her bedroom floor, and Helen's granddaughter is caught with the murder weapon in hand.

Sure of the girl's innocence, Helen embarks on a little investigation of her own and turns up plenty of folks who aren't grieving a bit now that Grace is dead . . .

# Not a Chance in Helen

*In the third River Road Mystery from USA Today bestselling author Susan McBride, Helen Evans knows her friend is not guilty of murder . . . She just has to prove it!*

When eighty-year-old Eleanora Duncan is found dead on her kitchen floor, Sheriff Frank Biddle suspects it isn't from natural causes. Eleanora wasn't exactly your average senior citizen. She was a widow worth millions, although all her money couldn't buy her happiness—not after losing both her husband and son.

Eleanora's bitterness alienated those around her, but did that bitterness make her the victim of foul play? Soon Jean Duncan, Eleanora's daughter-in-law, becomes the prime suspect. But the sheriff gets more than he bargained for when Helen Evans comes to the aid of her friend.

Helen knows that Jean didn't murder Eleanora, despite the very bad blood between them. So she uses every means at her disposal in order to clear Jean's name and track down Eleanora's killer.

## About the Author

**SUSAN McBRIDE** is the *USA Today* bestselling author of *Blue Blood*, the first of the Debutante Dropout Mysteries. The award-winning series includes *The Good Girl's Guide to Murder*, *The Lone Star Lonely Hearts Club*, *Night of the Living Deb*, *Too Pretty to Die*, and *Say Yes to the Death*. She's also the author of the River Road Mysteries—*To Helen Back*, *Mad as Helen*, *Not a Chance in Helen*, and *Come Helen High Water*—in addition to three works of women's fiction, *The Truth About Love and Lightning*, *Little Black Dress*, and *The Cougar Club*, all Target Recommended Reads. She lives in St. Louis, Missouri, with her husband and daughter.

Visit Susan's website at www.SusanMcBride.com for more info.

Discover great authors, exclusive offers, and more at hc.com.